AJ
PRINCESS of ORE
LOVE'S SECRET PLACE

FAITH O. ADIORHO

Ai

Princess of Ore

Love's Secret Place

Faith O. Adiorho

Copyright © 2024 Faith O Adiorho

Published by The Written Faith

TWF Books

Manchester, UK

https://thewrittenfaith.com/the-written-faith-books/

All rights reserved. No part of this publication may be reproduced, distributed, or transmitted in any form or by any means, including photocopying, recording, or other electronic or mechanical methods, without the prior written permission of the publisher.

For permission requests, use the contact form at https://thewrittenfaith.com/contact/.

The story, all names, characters, and incidents portrayed in this production are fictitious. No identification with actual persons (living or deceased), places, buildings, and products is intended or should be inferred.

Cover design by Nithin Abraham

Cover art by Deborah Agada

To my one true King, my Beloved, my All.

For my beloved mother, whose support is immeasurable; for my beloved Marija, who consistently pushes me into purpose; for Joy the only big sister I can call a best friend, for my dear cousin Essylorry, to whom I first told this story, and whose reactions changed the course of the book; for Tharmani, for Sinead, for Precious, for Annah & Alph, and for my beloved prodigy Afa-Maelle, who I believe will write world-renowned books.

PROLOGUE

Ai felt her head spin and her heart pound tumultuously, as fearsome thoughts beclouded her mind. She willed herself to be still, but her body disobeyed as it trembled with fright. Never in her short years of existence, had she been faced with such a deadly circumstance.

In the safety of the palace and surrounded by her many soldiers she never had reason to fear any form of assault. However, standing alone in the foreign orphanage she had been forbidden from visiting, she was naught, but a frail girl.

Shall this be my end? She pondered shakily with trepidation.

Five men towered over her, the edges of their swords glinting in the sunlight. For the first time, since he had been mandated into her service, she regretted not taking her lion-like personal guard into her confidence, as she did with Nathan.

She should have told him of her clandestine visits to the neglected orphanage, but his loyalty, she was certain, lay with the King. She could not risk being exposed for her defiant act against her father's clear instructions.

Perhaps I should have commanded him to keep it a secret; then, he would have been bound to obey my royal command.

It was quite useless and rather too late to regret her poor decisions. Even if he were with her, sworn to secrecy, the five bloodthirsty men that stood before her would have hacked him down before he could even unsheathe his sword. He would have died, and she would undoubtedly be next.

Nonetheless, Nathan, her sole friend in Ore, was the only person who knew of her whereabouts at that moment and since he was unaware of the dangers she was in, he was most unlikely to come to her aid. He was the third friend she had made after befriending two royal children at the defunct Yachad festival.

"Stay away from the princess!" A child's piercing voice tore through her thoughts. The young royal watched in dismay as several little orphan boys took positions, standing protectively in front of her.

She stared in consternation at the children, whose well-being had been the reason for her rebellion. She barely knew any of their names but had taken to doing her best to see them fed and educated in the short time she had with them each week.

Why would they not listen to me and remain in the reading room where they are safe?

One of the men with a raggedy-looking face and a large belly laughed scornfully, as he eyed the little one. "Ye brats are like ants under me feet. I shall crush ye if ye stand in me way."

"We shall never let you!" one of the boys exclaimed, approaching the men bravely.

"Shut ye mouth, boy," the man shouted angrily, stepping forward and assaulting the boy with a blow so hard that the child fell to the ground. The princess gasped in horror as some of the other children helped the boy stand.

"Please, do not hurt anyone on my account." She said, squeezing past the protesting children, with all fears forgotten. "What is it that you seek from me? Here I am, do not hurt the children."

The boys began protesting loudly, some going as far as yelling they would fight for her to their last.

"Silence!" A fiercely intimidating voice of another rogue rang through the old hall, causing all the children to fall quiet. He looked just as fierce as he sounded, with long hair, an eyepatch across one eye, and some scars on his scruffy bearded face. "You children are all useless to the kingdom, a burden if I may. No one shall mourn your deaths, so it shall be little work ridding Ore of you rats if it is what it takes to get to the nuisance girl."

"That, sir, will not be necessary," The princess declared feeling more strengthened by the willingness of such babes to lay down their lives for her when she had done so little for them. "There shall be no need to spill the blood of innocent children for my sake."

The children, now in floods of tears, pulled and grabbed at her, doing whatever they could to stop her from going to the men, hoping their combined strength could somehow shield her. She turned to them and spoke, "Do not fear, dear little ones, remember these words, 'There is no greater love than to lay one's life down for another."

The man with the eyepatch laughed wickedly, "Stop spewing nonsense, dark princess. Come quickly so I can end this. Your very existence is a shame to our kingdom."

His words were like a dagger piercing through her chest. She knew exactly what he meant, as she was not only an adoptive princess, but she also possessed features quite different from everyone else in the kingdom. From her dark complexion to the coiled texture of her hair, it was no surprise that she was despised as the sole princess of the Kingdom.

She had been born when her parents, the then prince and princess of Ore were returning from a diplomatic mission to a kingdom in the East of Asia with which Ore was in friendly relations. Their party had happened upon a pregnant woman lying on the side of the horse path, alone, but ready to deliver the child in her womb.

Her father, then Prince James, had commanded that they halt their journey to help the woman.

The woman birthed the child but did not survive the blood loss from delayed delivery. The prince gallantly swore to the dying woman to take the child as though it were his very own seed. He was certain their meeting was a divine chance to give him and his wife, the long-desired child they had spent so many years awaiting.

Ai's grandmother who had been a part of the diplomatic mission and a first-hand witness, told her the tale after she had pestered the woman into acquiescence. Since her parents always found a way to evade the questions of her birth, she found solace in hearing it from the woman's point of view.

Eva, the mother of the Queen, had an observable partiality for her granddaughter and was easily swayed to do her bidding. She told Ai that her name originated from the Nichi kingdom, from which they had been returning.

Prince James was crowned King of Ore a few weeks after they arrived from the mission since the previous king had died during his absence. It was during the celebration of his coronation, that the princess was presented to the people against the newly crowned Queen's fearful protest.

Her grandmother expressed that Queen Anne, Ai's mother feared that the people would have rioted if the highly revered prophet Asher had not immediately stepped forward and blessed her as a princess.

Since Ai had remained heavily guarded under her father's watch her whole life, it was no surprise that she was under attack, when she was alone and vulnerable. She slowly approached the ferocious-looking men. It was the man with the large stomach who raised his sword at her, and her eyes fluttered closed. She stood unafraid, awaiting her end, as she muttered her last prayers.

That end never came, as she was instead met with the sound of iron striking iron. Her eyes flew open, and she beheld the broad back and long dark hair of the man she had wished to appear since the ferocious men arrived at the orphanage. She inadvertently took a step back to observe that he had deflected the attack of the enemy's sword. Wherever he had come from was a mystery to her, but streams of joy bubbled in her heart at the sight of him.

In a brief suspended moment, he turned to her, and his rich forest green eyes locked on hers. In them were unspoken words of unquestionable assurance and fierce protection.

Although he was a single man against five bloodthirsty men, the princess had never felt as assured of safety as she did in his presence. She was unsure if it was because her father boasted of his physical prowess or the fact that he had appeared out of nowhere, but she was quite certain he would not let harm come to her.

In the next second, the sturdy soldier turned from her and skilfully unsheathed a dagger from his opponent's belt, thrusting it into his distended ale-rich stomach.

The other men, as stunned as Ai was, stood frozen in bewilderment, as their comrade dropped to the ground. The soldier however spared no time as he took advantage of their confusion. His sword was swift, and his movements agile. In a single slice motion, another man was taken down.

The third bandit was on the ground with the dagger in his chest in another moment, but the fourth seemed more skilled than the rest. It was the man with the eyepatch, whom she also assumed was the leader of the gang. He was able to engage her guard in an intense sword fight.

The princess watched as her protector used his feet to kick the fifth, who attempted to assist his comrade, sending him crashing against some empty barrels. He did this while maintaining a good fight against his formidable opponent.

Snapping out of her awe, the princess went into action, turning to the children whose safety was her priority. She urged them into the little reading room, where the others were, and received no objections as they looked horrified by what they had witnessed.

Although it was the first time the young royal had seen any person get killed, she knew she had to be strong for the children and resisted the urge to empty whatever was in her stomach at that moment.

After she had ensured the children were safely locked away, she turned back to the battle and saw the man who had been kicked against the barrels, rise with a stagger, and pull a dagger from the sheath strapped around his waist. She turned her eyes to see that her protector had just stabbed his opponent with his sword, which seemed quite deeply embedded in the man.

She doubted that he would have enough time to retrieve his weapon to defend himself, so she acted on impulse and ran towards him, throwing herself in between her dark-haired saviour and the impending attack.

However, before she could get struck, she felt the grip of firm hands on her shoulders and was urgently tossed out of harm's way. She staggered from the impact and by the time she regained balance she looked up to see her protector break the enemy's neck in one swift turn.

Despite the horrific sight before her, she breathed out in relief, gladdened that even though he had been outnumbered, her saviour emerged as the victor. It gave credence to all her father had claimed about him, and she could finally understand the King's insistence on making him her guard.

"Are you hurt, princess?" Her protector asked, turning slightly to her.

Ai shook her head vehemently, as several questions swamped her mind. The most prominent being her desire to know how he had found her as the chances that Nathan had divulged it to him were very slim.

"Jarit…" She began, but before she had the opportunity to utter the questions that plagued her, she was interrupted by his voice, which sounded hoarser than she recalled it to be.

"I do not like the name."

The princess blinked in confusion at his words, as she could not for the life of her understand how it signified in their current predicament.

She vaguely recalled asking a while before, if he liked his name. He had told her it meant 'iron fist', and admitted, nonchalantly, that it had been given when he was in the army, because of his skill. At that time, he had not responded to the question. It was quite odd that he chose such a time to answer.

She was just about to tell him her sentiments when she saw him stagger towards a pillar and rest his back. A cold feeling washed over her as she could behold from his side profile, a dagger lodged in his stomach area. She had the alarming realisation that he had been stabbed in her stead by the last thug.

"Jarit! Jarit…" She called, running towards him as his eyes drooped and he slowly slid down the pillar.

♦

ONE

Ai, the sole princess of Ore felt her heart drop in consternation, as she turned to see that she had been followed into her secret refuge. She wiped her teary eyes and turned to behold the youth with raven dark hair and shiny blue eyes staring down at her. He was much taller and looked older than she.

"Who are you and how did you find this place?" She asked, agitated.

"You ran into me a moment ago and I simply followed you here, " the boy declared proudly.

She vaguely recalled crashing into a person she assumed was an official from another kingdom, and had begged his pardon, before running off to her intended destination.

Her Secret Garden.

For the first time since her father gifted it to her, Ai appreciated the existence of the hidden refuge. It was a secret inner garden, camouflaged by an outer one and known only to a few trusted servants, who kept it groomed and tidy for her use. King James had presented it to her on the seventh anniversary of her birth. It took several years, but she eventually became familiar with the secret entrance and the secret passage within it that led out of the palace.

Her reason for being there at that time was to escape the scornful gazes of the guest princes and princesses who had been unkind to her, despite her being the host princess of the ongoing Yachad festival.

Unlike the Ore nobles, who regardless of their contempt dared not scorn her, the royals from other kingdoms were her peers and were not afraid to disregard her like she did not exist. Some princesses even dared to speak indiscreetly on their parents' warnings to avoid her for her peculiar complexion. She wished to heaven that she had not stepped out of her chambers that day.

Ai gazed dumbfounded at the boy before her for a moment, then inwardly acknowledged that her carelessness had made the unfamiliar youth discover the secret place.

"Why have you followed me here?"

"You stumbled into me looking troubled, and I followed to make sure all was well with you." She glanced up at him curiously, knowing she had never met any quite like him.

"Princess, Princess, you must awaken now."

Ai opened her eyes to the red-headed, **fair-faced** maidservant, whose **full lips held the widest smile and hazel eyes sparkled with excitement.**

"Forgive us, Your Highness, but you have slept longer than you usually do, and you do have that case at noon." Another voice in the room said. Ai looked beyond the smiling redhead, to the blond-haired and blue-eyed small woman, who was far beyond her thirtieth year and had such fair skin that made her look almost translucent. They were her trusted handmaidens whose loyalty she had no reason to doubt.

She sat up on her bed and smiled. "Do not let it bother you, dear Martha, I did have a captivating dream that kept me in slumber, and I thank you for waking me. Now, we must make haste for I wish to outwit that knight of mine today."

The two women curtsied and began to ready the princess for the day. Ai was not surprised that she had dreamed about the defunct Yachad festival, since it had beclouded her thoughts before she went to sleep the previous night.

The Yachad festival was a festival of great kingdoms, which Ore had hosted for two consecutive years. It was a meeting of sovereigns and royals to maintain a diplomatic balance and avoid wars. It had been discontinued in the second year due to a disagreement amongst the kings.

She had indeed met the dark-haired boy at the festival. After he discovered her garden, he also brought his sister to her. They spent most of their time together throughout the festivals and struck an intimate friendship.

The siblings referred to themselves as Sora and Hana which were also names from the Nichi kingdom. Sora had explained that they had visited the same kingdom when they were younger, and it was the names they were given. She had been contented with this and had not bothered to ask their real names until the festival was discontinued, and it was too late to do so.

Although she had discovered they were prince and princess, she was uncertain from what kingdom they hailed, since many kingdoms were represented at the Yachad festival. All she had of them was a letter Sora had sent to her through a palace guard before his departure. It was one of her most treasured possessions...

"Which of these dresses do you wish to wear, Your Highness?" Surina asked, pulling Ai out of retrospection. The princess barely glanced at the two dresses presented to her, before rising and walking to her vanity.

"Whichever one shall allow for swift and noiseless movements, if you please, dear Surina." She responded simply and allowed the two women to prepare her for the day.

Pleased with their work, she bid them goodbye and walked to the door. Ai held her breath as she quietly opened it and was gladdened to see no one in front of her chambers. However, on further inspection, she noticed the source of her agitation seated with his eyes closed and arms folded at the right side of the passage.

He had one leg bent towards himself, the other stretched out, and his back against a pillar. His sword was laid next to him, and he appeared to be asleep. Several locks of his short dark hair hovered over his forehead and past his closed lids. It was almost as though his face was glowing in the rise of the morning sun.

The princess observed his fair angular face for a moment and suddenly had a compulsive desire to capture him in a painting. The possibility of his remaining in that position long enough to be painted was however non-existent, and her immediate goal to slip away unnoticed was paramount. She acknowledged that the only way she could achieve such a feat was by avoiding him completely, using the longer path through the left side of the passage.

Ai pulled her gaze away from his compelling image and turned to the proposed path, observing with excitement that there were no palace guards around. She was certain she could easily execute her escape without interruption or embarrassment.

It was the day before the start of the Love Festival, and the palace was bustling with preparations for the grand celebration. It was the second festival held in Ore in the young royal's lifetime, and she looked forward to it with the hope of being reunited with her precious friends.

Ai shook her head to dismiss her thoughts, as her priority for the morning was to silently leave her room without being noticed. Her feet had barely crossed her door's threshold when the rich deep voice of her overly efficient knight came to her hearing.

"A very fine morning it is, your highness." The startled princess had to hold onto the door frame to keep from stumbling. She turned to see the fiery emerald orbs staring straight at her as though they had not been closed a moment ago.

Her knight's eyes had always been a source of awe to her. Although green eyes were not commonplace, they were also not too surprising or unique in Ore. There was however something different and unique about her knight that she could not place her finger on. It made her wonder if he possessed Asian roots or if he was even at all from this earthly plane. It was also what made her maids think he was the most handsome in Ore.

"I assumed you were taking a well-deserved and long-overdue nap, Michael." She responded, ignoring his questioning gaze, as she frowned and wondered over and again if he was human or a supernatural being.

"I expect you would have had me awakened if that was the case." He said, rising, and picking up his sword. "Except, it was your intention to slip away..."

"And why, sir, would I wish to do that?" she interrupted defensively, putting her hand on her waist as he approached her, looking everything like the supernatural being she supposed him to be, in the Ore military uniform.

"Perhaps, you wish to escape my tiresome presence." He responded, stopping right in front of her and staring down at her with a brow raised. The princess was considered a tall female, but before her knight, who stood almost two heads taller than she, it was as though she were a child.

She did not put it far from him to think of her as a child, as he was a little over five years older. She was aware that most were intimidated at the mere sight of him but she, on the contrary, did all in her power to intimidate him. It was all in futility, as he was the boldest and most courageous individual she had ever met. The fact that he stood almost two heads above her, was only one of the many pitfalls in her endeavour.

"I should have escaped, if you were not so odiously efficient!" She mumbled, squinting her eyes in a bid to give him a darting look. "I did not make a sound! How is it that you became aware of my presence?" The man smirked smugly, lifting his head.

"I believe your assumption that I was in a state of slumber was your first error."

"That is nonetheless of little significance since your eyes were closed, my door is noiseless, and so was I." Ai argued.

"Would it satisfy you if I told you that I could smell your presence, Your Highness?"

"No, it would not! I wear no strong scents."

"Well then, what shall I say that would be pleasing to you?"

"I have not asked you to tell me what I wish to hear, Michael. I get my fill of that from the palace servants." She responded with evident annoyance. "All I ask is that you tell me how it is that you have the supernatural ability to sense a person's presence regardless of the distance. As your princess, I demand that you tell me the truth and nothing less!"

There was a twinkling in his eyes that indicated that he was keeping himself from laughing.

"I have told you several times, but you always choose to disbelieve me. I have therefore resigned myself to saying whatever is pleasing to your hearing."

"The sad explanation of having all your senses alert is not very helpful to me now, is it? You ought to train me on how to achieve this by telling me every detail."

"It is not my duty to train you, Your Highness. I believe you have some other soldier in that respect." He stated grinning.

The princess thought of the skilful soldier her father had put in charge of her battle training, since the awful incident at the orphanage. She had long surpassed the middle-aged man's skill and was quite bored of sparring with him.

"You are my knight, and you should teach me!"

"My duty, dear princess, is to protect you."

"I should not need your protection, had I your skill, should I?"

"But how shameful would it be to our kingdom if our sole princess protected herself?" The knight responded, and Ai stumped her foot in childish annoyance.

"You know, you should have remained Jarit, for you are most certainly made of iron!" As soon as the words were out of her mouth, she noticed the man's smile vanish abruptly and wished she had not uttered them.

TWO

Ai swiftly placed her hands over her mouth, feeling regretful of her words as she recalled the events that led to the change of her Knight's name from Jarit to Michael.

After he had been stabbed at the orphanage, she had thought he was dead, but by some good fortune, he survived. When he awoke, after many days of lying unconscious, it seemed like he had been born anew, and the princess had the new name ready.

Calling his old name was tantamount to reminding him of the past in which he was a nameless soldier identified as Jarit because of his strength and physical prowess.

"Forgive me, princess," the knight said seriously.

"No, Michael, I beg your pardon. I should not have said it. Just, you were so provoking, and I became out of patience with your cool manners. I know you have long abandoned that name, but I have been so dim-witted to use it to offend you. I shiver whenever I recall that incident that led to the change of your name, and I cannot believe my foolishness. Do forgive me, please."

"That incident is almost seven years past. Do you not forget?"

"I wish I would, but I daresay I never shall, for you almost died..."

"I am very much alive, and you should be sorry I am for I have been naught but a nuisance to you." His smile had returned but at a cost.

"You must know that I do not find your words at all amusing. I will admit that the past few days of you following me everywhere have been very wearisome, but I should not know what I would do if you died. Oh, you must not die!" She insisted with a passion that caused the man to smirk.

"I have no intention to. I have the mind to remain alive and be a nuisance to you all the days of your life."

"Provoking tease! You are just as bad as Nathan!" She scoffed and turned in a huff towards her destination.

"Now, Your Highness, you insult me, comparing me to that puppy!" he responded, following behind her. "I see no reason you should continue on this long path since you have quite failed in your attempt to escape me." Ai stifled a giggle at his words but turned towards the correct path with her head raised high.

After the woeful orphanage incident, her allegiant guard survived thanks to the almost immediate arrival of her father and his soldiers on the scene after he lost consciousness.

She discovered that it was Nathan who had divulged her secret to Michael and her father but had been obliged to forgive him when he explained that her young guard had bullied the information out of him.

Michael had overheard some drunken men discuss a scheme against her the previous day but had not ascertained it, till he discovered from Nathan that she was indeed at the location of the plot. He had ordered Nathan to inform the king about it, whilst he went ahead to save her, hence their arrival on the scene, some minutes after the battle.

Her hero had remained unconscious for many days, and she sat at his side for most of her waking hours, reading aloud to him, as she did before the incident. Her face was therefore the first he beheld when he opened his eyes, and she had been so overjoyed that she forgot propriety and threw herself upon him weeping tears of joy. In his unconscious days, she had enough time to think up a 'befitting' name for him.

Michael.

The warring archangel of the Almighty God. No name suited him better. She had called him by the name after pulling herself from his chest, and he nodded with immediate understanding. His quick wit became a point of her amazement and amusement in the period that followed.

It took several months before he was perfectly healed and within that time, he became known by the name, Michael. He was made to remain within the palace and slowly struck a friendship with herself and Nathan. However, unlike Nathan, he never forgot the formality of their ranks, and although the princess gave him freedom to ensure they were as informal as they could be, he remained rigid.

After he was fully recovered, he was knighted by her father with the title *'Royal Protector of the Ore Princess.'*

Ai heaved a sigh as she arrived at the royal door of the elegantly designed throne room where she was to judge a case between two entitled nobles. All present, including several soldiers and court officials, bowed to her.

Michael took his place beside her as she sat on the throne-like chair prepared for her, beside the ones belonging to her parents. Although his duties were not usually imposing, he was under direct orders from the King to remain at her side for the duration of the Love Festival, which happened to end on the twenty-first anniversary of her birth.

Even when her father refused to admit it, Ai knew the main reason for the Love festival, coincidentally named after her was that she was entering the age of her majority. One thing he did not deny was that the ball, which was to be on the last day of the festival, and the anniversary of her birth, was specifically in her honour.

The princess gave the order for the case to begin and in a few moments, as she expected, she was resisting the strong urge to yawn as the two nobles before her bickered on.

She wished her father would permit her to handle more interesting cases, like those from the commoners, but since he only thought her safe amongst the nobles, she was laden with the burden of settling the disputes of such conceited men.

These same egotistic men had the responsibility of settling the disputes of commoners, and Ai shuddered at the thought of how her people were treated.

"What do you say to this, your highness? The only thing that indicates the boundaries of our lands is that old map. My servants must have planted my crops on the part of the land he claims as his own. I cannot blame them, for no one, I assure you, looks at the map before they plant. Sir Marlow however, refuses to allow my crops to grow till harvest, after which I shall happily remove from his land." The middle-aged nobleman stated.

The princess was diverted by his balding head which was poorly covered by a wig. She wondered in amusement if it would fall off since it kept moving as the man continued gesticulating.

"Your Highness, it is only just that I claim that which is rightfully mine, regardless of who has used it. It is Sir Crita's loss for not observing the map before encroaching on my land." The other noble scoffed in response, pulling her attention to him. He looked like his rival, with his bald head and heavily rounded gut. In her opinion, most of the lower-class nobles past their sixtieth summer bore similar features and she could hardly tell them apart.

"Your Highness, I do not deny that Sir Marlow owns the land. But it shall be most unjust to allow his serfs to reap the harvest of the labour of my men."

"Shall it be just if my men were to destroy your crops?" This response from Sir Marlow only had the effect of angering his rival and it became a heated argument between them, that was only quelled when the princess lifted her hand. She knew if she let them bicker on, she would end up with a headache.

"May I see the map of your lands?" She asked, and without awaiting the consent of the nobles, a palace guard retrieved it and handed it to her.

Ai studied it with a frown, as she recognised the details on the parchment. A similar map lay in her study, but it outlined a land belonging to the throne. It was the one with which the complainant shared boundaries. A land her father had given her jurisdiction over, which she had been planning to use as a public field where the poor could glean from its food crops. She had gotten reports that a noble had encroached on the land and had been considering taking action to remove him.

Ai looked up from the map and at the two eager faces as they both anticipated her verdict. She considered addressing Sir Marlor's encroachment but feared the look of displeasure she would receive in return.

Whenever she gave any unfavourable verdict, a look of disapproval always followed, leaving her feeling unwanted. All she desired was to be accepted by her people, but angering the nobles with strict and objective verdicts only seemed to put a gulf between her and that goal. She therefore always strived to maintain impartiality in such a way that left all parties pleased.

"Sir Marlow, I shall offer you double the equivalent plot that Sir Crita has encroached on, from the royal field that borders your land. This shall become a replacement for your land. This will be so on the condition that hedges be built around, to avoid further disputes." Ai was gladdened by the looks of approval following her offer.

What the men did not know, was that she only intended to give Sir Marlow the part of the land he already occupied. She indicated to one of the officials how the borders would be divided on the map. Although Ai was happy that she had avoided the displeasure of the men, the thought that such an agreement was detrimental to her plans which could benefit all of Ore's citizens, especially the commoners, was difficult to bear.

"My knight shall see you to the palace gates and assign someone suitable to supervise this verdict," she announced, turning to Michael with a mischievous smile. She ignored the question in his eyes and rose from her seat. She was most certain that he had deduced her plans, but obeyed her order, nonetheless. The two nobles bowed, looking discomfited as Michael walked towards them, towering over them. His intimidating presence had an effect that made even the wealthiest nobles cower, especially with the widespread knowledge of his physical prowess.

As the men were led out of the throne room, Ai slipped out through the private backdoor designed for the royals to enter and exit the room. She resisted the urge to run, as the palace guards and servants bowed to her.

She could hardly contain her excitement at the chance to win the hide-and-seek game she had begun and forced the knight into. She had but a few minutes, before he came in pursuit of her, and she intended to have at least an hour out of his presence. Whilst she could not boast of outwitting him, she had found a way to escape him, using his weakness against him. One that made him never defy her orders in the presence of others.

His gallant allegiance.

THREE

Ai walked gracefully to her father's library, mindful that Michael would never seek her there. The guards bowed to her and opened the doors, with no questions, as they were acquainted with her freely visiting her father since she was a child. She hardly ever needed an announcement or permission to enter his presence. She stopped at a large mirror on the path into the inner study.

She was quite content with the choice of attire handpicked by her two trusted handmaidens. It was a pink dress with black lace at the hems which magnificently portrayed her slim figure, and boldly depicted her royal status. She was often told how her facial features made her appear much younger than the twenty years she had lived. She had thick lashes that framed her deep brown eyes, a small nose, and full lips of dark brown outer edges which blended seamlessly with the light pink in the centre.

She allowed her eyes to trail to her full hair, brushed away from her face and put in a braid that encircled her head. The unusual texture of her hair **was one of the most daunting tasks in her daily preparation.**

Martha, who had served her from her childhood, and Surina who had entered her service in her teenage years, were the only people, **besides her mother,** who had successfully perfected the art of manoeuvring the defiant mass atop her head. They were the only handmaidens whose loyalty she never doubted.

A diadem had been placed on her head by Surina to 'intimidate the greedy nobles' as she claimed. Ai sighed, as intimidation was the last thing she intended to do. She could, however, not but agree that it did signify her royal position, as she had opted to wear a simple pearl necklace and small pearl earrings. Unlike when she was younger, she did not particularly like jewellery, as they were heavy and tiresome and had done nothing to earn her friendships. Ai's shapely brows dipped into a frown, as she stared at her image. The thought that recurred most frequently in her mind, made an appearance again.

Had I been of a fairer complexion, I would have been regarded as a great beauty.

She was quick to shake it off, when she recalled the first time, she had erroneously voiced it out to her mother. Although the queen had scolded and reassured her that she was beautiful, she realised that her words had a dampening effect on the woman.

Queen Anne blamed her regular scolding for her daughter's feeling of inferiority, expressing that she had failed as a mother. It took several weeks for Ai to convince the woman that she had never felt neglected by her, nor had her methods of discipline made her feel any less loved.

The very memory of the mournful countenance her mother had in those painful weeks, was enough to make the princess shudder. She had never again uttered a negative comment against herself since that time. It was her good fortune that her father had been away in a different region at the time, and she had been able to convince her mother never to mention it to the man.

If her mother, who was the less doting parent had undergone such a mournful time because of such a statement, she feared to see the reaction of her father. Ai pulled her gaze away from her image and walked silently towards where she knew the king could be found.

King James, who was seated at his large table looking over a parchment, looked up as soon as he heard her enter and smiled warmly. His blue eyes sparkled beautifully, and he looked much younger than his eight and fifty years of age.

"Father," She greeted with a curtsy, returning his smile.

"My dearest Ai, what a good pleasure!" he said, rising and walking up to her, with his arms stretched. "You may ask anything you desire for the anniversary of your birth. Be it up to half of my kingdom, I shall gladly grant it unto you,"

"Father, how is it, that you ask this of me every year?" Ai giggled, putting her hands in his.

"My dear child, you have grown both in wisdom and grace and I tell you, I have the mind to give you all I own, for you are my joy and pride," he replied with a broad smile as she kissed his bearded cheek.

"If you truly mean this, then grant me the promise that you and Mother shall live a very long and healthy life." Her expressively pleased parent laughed loudly and heartily.

"You say this every year, child. It is yet time you become wittier in your requests."

"On this matter, I shall never concede, for it shall remain my sole desire evermore."

The princess had never had a reason to doubt the devotion and affection of her parents and reciprocated it greatly. It was the main reason she desired acceptance in the kingdom.

"Whatever is this emotional moment that I have yet again been excluded from?" Her mother's voice echoed through the room.

The queen, petite in comparison to her father's tall form, looked as beautiful as ever in her blue, heavily embroidered dress. Not a strand of her honey-brown hair was out of place, and although she was three and fifty, her beauty had not waned with age, for she looked not a day above thirty. Her grey-blue eyes trailed critically over her daughter.

"How do you do, Mother?" The princess greeted, with a graceful curtsy.

"Ai, I had the joy of running into your knight on my way here. Whilst I did not put him in the uncomfortable position of asking your whereabouts, I could tell that he was in search of you. Could it be that you are here to evade his presence?"

Ai sighed in defeat, as her mother began a lecture on how unbecoming it was to escape the one whose sole aim was to protect her.

She decided that her next best option was to return to her chambers without getting found by her knight. Although it would not be such a flawless victory, it would still mean that she had evaded him, nonetheless. Her only trouble was walking to her chambers, without being found by the supernatural knight.

"Dear child, do you hear anything I say?" Her mother's raised voice tore through her thoughts. She had not been attending to her words but had caught on to a few things she had said about the dangers of being alone in such festive times.

"Yes, Mother. I shall go now to him."

"Your knight is the only man we can trust to keep you safe. You will just have to bear with his persistent presence until the end of the celebrations. We are aware of your impulsive tendencies and would rather not have a repeat of the orphanage incident." Her mother added, in a warning tone.

"Rest assured, Mother, there shall be no repeat of it."

The younger royal excused herself and walked out of the library, taking a longer route to her chambers in the hope that her knight would not find her. She did her best to ignore how deeply her mother's words affected her, but it weighed heavily on her mind. The queen said it to remind her of the consequences of defying their instructions since she had been expressly forbidden from visiting that orphanage at the time of the incident.

There were two orphanages in the Kingdom. One was specifically designed for known or proven Ore natives, and another was for foreign and unidentified children. Ai had visited the Ore orphanage for natives several times and was impressed with the way it was run.

Obstacles and resistance, most especially from her parents, had prevented her from visiting the foreign one, but the plight of the foreign orphans struck close to her heart as she felt she was quite like them. She sought an opportunity to locate the orphanage and visit the poor children.

The opportunity came with her friend Nathan, the adoptive son of the Prophet Asher. She had met him when he moved into the palace, after the Yachad festival. He became the third friend she ever made, and as soon as they were close enough to form a trusting friendship, the princess sent him off to find the Orphanage. He was able to locate it within a week, as his late mother had served the children before her demise.

Ai was forced to visit clandestinely through her secret garden, which also had a hidden route that led out of the palace. Her accomplice accompanied her the first time and then provided her with a map and a horse for her consequent visits.

She had wept the first time she visited the old cold building, which leant precariously as though a mere gust of wind could send it sprawling. Its rickety, dilapidated doors did little to keep the elements out, and the place lacked basic amenities. The children...

Oh, the children... Malnourished, underfed, scrawny...

It was her love for the children that made her visits so frequent. She had at first visited once each month, but soon her visits became a weekly task. It was at the time when she frequented the orphanage that Michael had come into her service. She had met him a day after the anniversary of her fourteenth year. King James had decided that she needed optimum protection and requested the best soldier from Ore's Army.

Ai was introduced to the tall brawny man who was said to be the most qualified to protect the princess. The man had his head bowed the whole time, obscuring his features. He had gained no favour with her, for he seemed too stiff, as he followed every order given. In her opinion, he was a boy who had only seen nineteen summers, and she believed him rather too young to be considered the best.

She took her sentiments before her father, expressing that a youth, who had not attained his majority could hardly offer the level of protection he desired for his daughter. Her father waved off her concerns and expressed that he had seen the youth in actual combat and had no doubt he was the right one for the job.

At the time, she had resented having a personal guard, because she wished to protect her clandestine visits to the orphanage. Her resentment however turned into curiosity, as the man did not spy on her as she thought he would. He gave Ai the impression that he resented being her guard as much as she did, as he had made it a point never to meet her eyes. He was forever bowing his head in her presence, and she made it her amusing goal to see that he lifted his eyes to hers of his own will. Most of her mischievous plans failed as the man was stoic, efficient and always saw through all her tricks.

Since at the time, he was only to serve her in the day from noon till sunset, she ran out of her futile tricks. She had even embroiled the unwilling Nathan in her plans, and yet still failed to make the man catch her eyes.

She learnt from her father that he was so good that he could still be as effective if he was blind. Her father was ever boasting of his skills, expressing that he had watched him spar with the commander of the Ore's army and was almost able to conquer the man regarded as Ore's strongest.

By the third week of his attending to her, she had given up on her efforts and settled for gazing upon his dark hair. It reminded her of her dark-haired friends, and she sometimes imagined he was Sora.

It was at an unexpected time, when she ceased trying, that she finally achieved her desire. She had long abandoned trying to see the man's face and went about reading the Holy Book, as instructed by Prophet Asher. It was a letter of an apostle to the Romans, and she found that she could grasp it better when she read aloud and had done so, ignoring the presence of the stoic young guard who stood at the door.

She had been oblivious that her reading had piqued his interest till the third day of her reading, his curiosity got the better of him. She had been reading the eighth chapter about a love that seemed so incredible that the man had taken a step forward and spoken.

"Surely you know such love could never exist!" He had proclaimed. It was the first time their eyes met, and she was so stunned by his fierce green eyes that she was wrought speechless. His staunch exterior flitted for a moment and what oddly seemed to be mutual surprise danced across his face.

Time seemed to have been suspended, as they stayed for several moments staring into each other's eyes. Then, reality cruelly tore apart the moment, and awkwardness filled the room. The man seemed to have shocked himself by acting in such a manner that was evidently out of his character and begged her pardon.

The princess was quick to wave off his apology and take advantage of his odd display of emotions. Unwilling to miss the moment, she engaged him in discussing what she had been reading. She acknowledged that she too had difficulty believing it the first time she read it. But that very chapter had become her favourite as it spoke of adoption, a topic she dearly wished to understand. She admitted that it was almost as though it was written for her benefit, and she had the mind to ask the Prophet to give her a better understanding of it.

The guard uttered a few words that day, but from that moment on, the stiff bowing and stubborn formalities were abandoned. Instead, he often stared into her eyes till she had to turn away. A lot of times she had to remind herself not to be intimidated by that beautiful mossy gaze. She had become determined to make a friend out of him but was always met with rigid formality. Although he listened as she read the Holy book, he never asked any questions, so the princess took it upon herself to ask him questions.

It was during one of her one-sided interviews she had asked the origin of his name and a few days later, the orphanage incident happened. After he risked his life for her, she took it upon herself to not only care for him but also befriend him, as he slowly recovered from his wounds. She went to see him daily and, on his request, she read the Holy Book to him.

Ai's recollection ended abruptly as she collided with a person. She had been so caught up in her memories that she failed to keep her eyes on the path she was walking. She was about to give her flustered apologies when she looked up and saw the familiar smug smile, she had become accustomed to.

"Nathan." She observed dryly.

FOUR

The tall man, whose pleasant-looking face did little to hide his Asian roots, grinned widely at her, revealing a set of perfectly placed teeth. His small dark eyes became lit up with a mischievous glint as he ran his fingers through his short brown hair. The princess had no doubt that he had seen her and yet allowed her to run into him.

"A princess with her head always in the cloud. Whatever shall be done with you?" He quipped.

"Perhaps more room shall be made, so that I may continue on my way,"

"And miss the sour look on your face? Nay! Besides, I shall have you know that I may have saved you from walking into a wall. Seeing as you walked right into me, what is to say that you would not walk into an inanimate object."

The princess, unable to come up with an appropriate response, sighed and begrudgingly agreed. In truth, she had been so lost in her reminiscing thoughts that she had not at all noticed him. Thankfully, he was the only person with whom she never felt embarrassed.

Her most trusted friend.

Ai had met him in the same year that the Yachad festival ended when he suddenly moved into the palace's chapel. The fact that he, just like herself, had distinguishing features from the people of Ore made him an attractive prospect for friendship. Prophet Asher told her of his background and the reason for taking him in.

His parents were ambassadors from the Nichi Kingdom who lived in Ore. When his father died because of an illness, his mother chose to remain in Ore with her young son. She had used her resources to help the children in the foreign orphanage and helped Prophet Asher wherever she could.

Ai had met the kind woman only once at the Prophet's office, and her warm smile that held no judgment had stood out to the princess. The woman had honoured her as a royal but had not looked contemptuously at her as other nobles did.

It was another reason she had been endeared to Nathan, even though she only met him after his mother passed away. He had lost his mother to an illness at the age of fifteen, and the

Prophet adopted him as a son and brought him to live in the palace.

The first day Ai had seen him, she had gone for her weekly teachings of the Holy Book and Nathan had been present in Prophet Asher's study, looking gloomy. At the time, her first thought was that his skin was not as pale as everyone she knew, and his almond-shaped eyes were small and unique. From that time, she had done all to make him feel at home in the palace, and although he seemed suspicious of her kindness, in less than a month he became more at ease with her as they learned the Holy Book together. Not once did he question her complexion or features. Several months later, he became her most trusted peer and the biggest jokester she ever met, taunting her in the most creative, but good-natured way.

"Ai!" The sound of her name and the snapping of fingers pulled her to the present. She observed her friend staring down at her with a frown. "Are you unwell? How much shall it cost to share such engaging thoughts that have made you so lost, even in my presence?"

The princess smiled up at him. "It is quite dim-witted to assume I shall, even for the most priceless jewel, share my thoughts with a man who has no regard for my nerves." This response caused the look of concern on Nathan's face to vanish and be replaced with his usual smug look.

"Well, I am quite certain your foolish thoughts would be nothing worth more than a copper coin."

The princess was compelled to hold back her clever retort, as the sound of a small cough behind her, caused her to stiffen.

"I have sought you everywhere princess," The rich deep voice of her knight reverberated and ricocheted through the passage. Ai scowled at Nathan, faulting him on her insides for foiling her plans. "Could it be that this is all a part of your purposeful plan to rid yourself of my presence?"

Ai turned around to him, smiling sweetly. "Whatever has put that idea in your head, dear Michael?" She asked in a sing-song voice, but the look on the knight's face and his raised brow told that he was aware of all her antics. "Oh, please Michael, spare me the disapproving glare. I have had enough scolding from my mother on your account. I shall own that it was indeed my intention to be away from your clutches for at least an hour, but there is no escaping you now, is there?"

The knight took some steps towards her, and smiled, "I am aware of how painfully protective and imposing I have been on you these past few days, but you must understand that it shall only be but for a short time. You must suffer my presence, until the festivities are ended, and the palace is not open to every strange person who could cause you harm. I do not know if it was a purposeful plan of his majesty to end the festival with the celebration of your birth, but you shall surely be the centre of attention. Till then, you shall sadly have to endure, my close watchful eye, after which you may roam as freely as you were used to before the festival."

Ai gave him an apathetic look, "Tell me, sir, have you rehearsed that speech, or have you been around my mother for too long? For I am quite certain she said the same words to me a few moments ago." Nathan began to snicker and before Michael could utter the clever response the princess was certain he would have, she spoke again. "Please Michael, do not reprove me any further, for you are fast becoming a boring old man. I shall return to my chambers where I am the safest."

With a pivot of her small heels, she turned around and marched past Nathan, a smile fixed on her face as her mind devised another plan to escape her knight. She could only wonder how long she could keep up the amusing hide-and-seek game with her skilled knight, but she intended to enjoy every moment of it.

She could hear the two men, following closely behind, but kept her face fixed on her path, knowing that if she gave in to the strong desire to converse with them, it would ruin the tough facade she had displayed earlier.

"I beseech you Ai, do listen to Michael. I hear that people from other great kingdoms shall be in attendance. This includes their nobles and royals, who have no allegiance to you, and will doubtlessly endanger your life to get whatever they want." Nathan stated from behind her, concern heavy in his tone.

"What is this? The loyal accomplice performs a sad betrayal." Michael stated sardonically.

"Oh, hush Michael, if you think for a moment that I have allied with you, you must have maggots in your head. My allegiance is for the safety of the princess of my kingdom." Nathan responded defensively.

The princess ceased listening to them, as Nathan's words about other kingdoms presented her with the image of her long-lost friends. If they longed to see her as much as she did them, there was a high possibility that they would attend the festival. Her heart bubbled in excitement at the thought of meeting her first friends again. She would finally be able to ask whatever it was that letter in her possession meant. Most importantly, she would come to the knowledge of their real identities and their kingdom.

Ai spent the rest of the day resting in her chambers and planning on the best way to evade Michael, along with her maidservants. She took herself off to sleep early, eager and excited about her plan and the festival the next day.

She awoke the next morning before sunrise, ready to execute what she thought was a brilliant idea. She dressed herself in the blue gown that Surina had laid out the previous night. Although she found it difficult to ready herself without any aid, she was able to achieve a pleasing result. She was seated at her vanity, combing out her damp hair, when Martha walked in.

"Your Highness, you should not do these things yourself, please, allow me," Ai obliged the handmaiden since she was unsure of what style would be fitting for the day.

Within herself, she strongly desired to see all the bustling celebrations outside the palace but would not dare defy her father again. Her parents had been quite lenient with her after the orphanage incident, expressing that her experience was the greatest punishment. They even pitied her enough to stay by her through the first few nights after the incident, as she was forever having nightmares. She was certain they would not be as lenient if she did anything so foolish again.

"Is your husband well, Martha?" Ai asked, looking in the mirror to catch Martha's reaction. She giggled as she saw the woman blush, even in the candlelight. Teasing the woman had become a pastime amusement and a good distraction for her. "Tell me, are you still in love, or have you become bored?"

"Your Highness!" Martha exclaimed, as her face reddened in embarrassment. "My Marco is as healthy as ever. I still love him as though we were just wed. How could I be bored when we have just..." Martha ceased speaking as soon as she noticed that the princess was giggling. "Oh, dear princess, why do you tease me so? I know you're trying to put me to the blush."

"Why, Martha, you do me injustice if you think I am just funning. I am quite hopeful to understand this feeling of love that I have read so much about, and you, my lady, are my test subject," she responded, trying her utmost to suppress the urge to giggle some more at the look of pride that graced her handmaiden's face.

"I must say, my dear princess, that I am not the best authority on the subject, but I can only assure you that it is most pleasant to be in love. Now, Your Highness I see, you are laughing at me. Well, I shall never take any offence, for we are indebted to you," Martha responded, and Ai ceased from her giggles.

"Please Martha, do not speak like that, it is no fun when you do. I can assure you that you owe me nothing." Ai responded, wishing she had not begun the topic.

Martha had made it a duty to sing songs of thanksgiving to her for the unprecedented leave she granted her to be married, despite being a royal handmaiden. She was the first palace servant to be allowed to marry.

As soon as the princess had discovered that the woman had been infatuated with a chef in the palace, she had given permission for them to be wed. Some of the senior palace officers had been against this, but Ai easily won the approval of her parents, and the marriage had been granted.

The princess looked approvingly at her reflection in the mirror and nodded at the way her hair was styled. She arose and was about to step out when the older woman called her attention.

"You must have noticed that I came earlier than usual. Well, it is so that I may tell you discreetly without that tattle box, Surina around, that I, Your Highness, am with child." The princess stood stunned for a moment as she slowly took in the news, then threw her hands around the woman with profound joy.

"Dearest Martha, I am so happy to hear this. Ask anything of me and you shall have it! What shall I do? What shall I give you? Oh, what a silly question to ask, surely you shall require some time away, and so many things for the baby."

"No, Your Highness, I require nothing of you. You have done more than I could ever ask. I have told you now, only because Marco and I wished that you would be the first to know." the flustered woman cried out.

"My dear Martha, you cannot ask me to do nothing, for I shall never listen to such nonsense. Oh, what exciting news!" Ai exclaimed excitedly. Before the woman could respond, the princess recalled the reason she had awoken at such an early hour. "I must go now, Martha, we shall speak more on this matter next time." With that, she was off and out of her chambers.

The princess looked to the left and right and was quite pleased that Michael was nowhere in view. She walked merrily, down the passage, with a plan to watch the sunrise from her secret garden. She hoped to remain there for a long while, till she was certain that she had avoided the watchful bedazzling eyes of her knight, for at least an hour.

She hoped he would be sick with worry over losing her and was even more motivated by her imagination of his flustered face when she finally returned. However, as she turned around a bend in the passage, she saw him in the distance speaking to a palace guard and immediately turned around to use a different path. She placed a hand on her racing heart, as she wondered if he had seen her.

"Princess?" She heard him call out, answering her mental question.

Ai could not help the mischievous grin that crept onto her face. She grabbed her skirts and began to run towards her garden. Michael had been at the far end of the other passage and even with his speed, it would take him a while to catch up to her, especially with the tricky turns and bends she was taking to her destination.

As she ran through the main garden, she turned around to see if Michael was behind her and rejoiced within herself when she found that she successfully outran him. However, by the time she turned around, it was too late to avoid colliding with a person standing in her path.

Thankfully for her, the man was strong enough to withstand the impact. She, on the other hand, found herself falling and would have hit the ground if the strong arm of the man had not caught her around her shoulders right before. The princess, supposing him to be a palace guard, let out a heavy breath of relief, and began to thank him as he steadied her.

"It is no problem, miss..." the man began, but stopped mid-sentence, as soon as he was able to observe her. Ai blinked several times, bemused, not only because he had stopped so abruptly and was staring intensely at her, but also because she realised that he was neither a palace guard nor a person she was acquainted with.

FIVE

Ai struggled to examine the features of the man before her in the rising sunlight and she could tell from the little she saw that he was an unquestionably handsome young man. He seemed almost as tall as Michael and had an athletic build, which his attire could not conceal. His appearance was simple, and she deduced he was a commoner since no noble would wear such ordinary clothes.

She was certain she had never met him before then, and by the stunned look on his face, that he was not a servant in the palace. She was well acquainted with looks of surprise at her first meeting with anyone. Her complexion was not commonplace, and it was possibly his first time seeing anyone like her. Ai cleared her throat causing the man to blink, as though awoken from a trance.

"I beg your pardon," the man said, looking flustered that he had been caught staring. "You must be the princess Ai," he said, bowing his head to her. Since he honoured her that way, she became certain he was a commoner from Ore, who had been allowed entry into the palace.

"Please sir, lift your head. I am quite at fault, and I beg your pardon."

"No, Your Highness. I was distracted and I am to blame." The princess stared at him incredulously. She wondered how he could be at fault when all he did was stand, but withheld her opinion as she perceived it would only lead to a silly discourse.

"I assume you are here for the festival," she said instead with a small smile. The man lifted his head and stared at her for what seemed like an age, and she did all to ignore the dreadful feeling that he was thinking the worst of her as he gazed upon her in scrutiny. "May I ask why you are here in the garden at such an early hour?" It was an attempt to begin a conversation, but it had an unintended effect.

"Forgive me, Your Highness, have I trespassed?"

"No!" Ai responded with urgency, mortified that he would think she was conceited. "Please sir, let your mind be at ease, I believe this garden is open to all our guests from the festival." She expressed reassuringly, deciding to abandon her plans to get through to her secret garden, which was just beyond the hedge of the open one. "I do not intend to be a hindrance to you sir..." she began, only to be interrupted by the surprised voice of the man.

"Not at all, Your Highness, the contrary is the case, it is rather an honour to be in your presence. It is I who should ask if I am in your way since the garden is yours. I would, however, humbly dare to ask if I may remain. You have my promise to not be a nuisance to you."

Ai's breath caught in her throat, she rarely met anyone speak or act towards her in such an honouring manner on first meeting, and without her parents present. Since none could ask a princess to leave, they usually found incredible excuses to be away from her, even when she insisted that they stay.

In this case, the man had not made a move to leave, and it reminded her of her first friend, who had gone after her on their first meeting. She wondered if all the commoners of Ore were like the man before her, and wished her father would give her the liberty to communicate with them.

"Please sir, have it your way, I doubt you shall be a nuisance in such a large garden. Well, except you intend to pick out all the flowers–" She began but ceased speaking, as she recalled that she was jesting with a stranger. Her family and friends were acquainted with her jesting, but she had forgotten herself enough to speak to a stranger as though he was Nathan.

To her surprise, the man laughed out loud, apparently understanding her humour. Ai stared at him in awe as he laughed, even in the dim morning light she could observe that he was a most beautiful man, enough to rival Michael, *Ore's most handsome gentleman*, as Surina had incessantly claimed he was called within the kingdom. Even Nathan's angelic looks could not be compared to this man. She was almost mesmerised but got a hold of herself as he ceased laughing and smiled at her.

"I most certainly shall not do that, Your Highness. You have my word, that your flowers are safe," he replied, smiling, as he stared down at her.

Before she had the chance to think up any response, he bowed and excused himself, walking further through the garden. Ai stood still, unable to comprehend all that had just happened. She couldn't help the excitement bubbling in her belly, as she began to wonder if there were other people like the kind stranger in the festival.

She decided to return to her chambers since she was certain that Michael would find her out in a few moments. She encountered him on her way back.

"Princess Ai…" he began.

"Oh, please spare me, Michael, I am quite safe."

The devoted knight sighed and walked behind her as she strolled absently towards her chambers. She vaguely registered that he was explaining what was put in place for her safety throughout the festival.

Ai nodded but hardly heard anything he said as she thought back to what had just happened in the garden. Her thoughts ended abruptly when she noticed Michael had stopped talking. Turning to him, she saw that he was looking at her with concern. She laughed awkwardly, knowing he had noticed she was not attending to his words.

"Are you well, Your Highness? Did something happen when you ran off?" The princess froze and blinked repeatedly and began to stutter. She did not know how he could be so quick-witted.

"Nothing out of the ordinary…" She started, but thought again, as meeting a commoner was most unusual for her. The knight raised a brow, and Ai felt like a child under his questioning gaze, as she thought of ways to avoid answering. She was certain he would not like her encounter with the stranger and would give her a lecture. Fortunately, their overly cheerful friend came around, interrupting the subtle interrogation.

"Ai, what a surprise to see you up and out of your chambers at this time." The sunlight had become bright enough to see the large smug grin on Nathan's face, and Ai knew his rather annoying jesting was imminent.

"Nathan, I am aware that you are devising methods to amuse yourself at my expense, but I must speak to you about a serious matter." She said and was pleased with the look of curiosity that graced his face. She took him by the arm and attempted to walk away from her knight, but he only followed behind.

"Michael, may I have a private moment with Nathan?"

"No, you may not. If at all you paid heed to anything I said moments ago, you would know that passages are one of the…"

"Goodness! I shall not survive another boring lecture from you, good sir. I believe I shall be forced to tell you what I encountered in the garden since you are never going to let me off. Only promise, that you shall not give me a scolding, for I could never bear your boring scolds."

"Now, you know I shall not dare scold you, princess."

"No, you shan't, but you equally give the most boring lectures that could make anyone desire the rod instead," Nathan responded and earned a smack behind his head.

"Michael, take care, for one day you shall kill Nathan if you keep hitting his head that way." The princess expressed, looking with concern at her friend who was holding his assaulted head. His hands dropped swiftly as soon as she said this, and he eyed her incredulously.

"What a fragile creature you must think I am, Ai!"

"Well, you are not half as strong as Michael, and you do look like you would swoon at any moment." She said with a giggle. She turned to Michael before Nathan could retort. "Well good sir, it is just as Nathan says, and I neither desire a scolding, nor a lecture. Now, do I have your word?"

The bigger man observed her. She knew he was not naturally curious, but when it came to her safety, he was thorough. In truth, she did not desire to hide anything from him. He was the one man she trusted the most with her life.

"Well?" She pressed, watching as he sighed and ran his fingers through his hair.

"You have my word." He responded, doing little to hide his reluctance.

The princess grinned from side to side, pleased she would be spared a well-deserved speech on the dangers of treading the palace by herself. She led the men to her more discreet library where she disclosed the events of the morning. She made sure to emphasise how the stranger had caught her and possibly saved her from hitting her head on a stone and dying, proving he was no danger.

"Surely, you know that I shall steady you if you are falling. I just have not had the opportunity. I do not know why it is so much of a great matter that a stranger offered you help that should be natural to any man." Nathan said, scratching his head, and looking flustered.

"But Nathan, he was so agreeable and wonderful," Ai said dreamily, twirling, till she ended up right before her knight. She stared at his broad chest for a moment, before looking up into his unimpressed eyes. "He did not bring me any harm, Michael. He saved me from hurting myself." She said defensively.

"I understand your sentiments, your highness. What I cannot comprehend is how this common stranger gained access to the palace gardens at that time of the morning. Only a few Ore noblemen have access to the palace before noon when activities commence." The knight explained, thoughtfully.

Ai frowned, unwilling to accept the idea that the stranger could be a suspicious person. She remembered how good it felt to be accepted by him on the first encounter. "Perhaps, he is a servant whom I failed to recognise. I could not make out all his features from the dimness of the rising sun."

The soldier looked down at her, evidently dissatisfied with her assumption. "I gave my word to avoid giving you a lecture, but shall I at least have your word that you shall not repeat such mischievous acts?"

"No, you shall not!"

"Princess—"

"Surely Michael, you do not expect that I shall give you my word, simply because you gave yours. That, my dear friend, shall be the most ridiculous thing ever!"

"It shall indeed!" Nathan corroborated, nodding, but stepped out of the Knight's reach to avoid being hit again.

"I do not ask on that account. I only ask for your safety. The man you met could have been a rogue of some sort and—" Michael abruptly ceased speaking, as though realising that he had almost broken his word. The princess and Nathan broke into a round of laughter at this.

"I must say, Ai, that I am quite impressed that you foresaw this and avoided it," Nathan said after they ceased laughing.

"Well, I knew for a fact that a lecture or long speech was impending and had to outwit Michael somehow."

Nathan began laughing again. "Oh, how the mighty is fallen!" He exclaimed, and somehow failed to dodge the slap on his back that made him stagger. He turned to his attacker with a frown. "I shall one day die at your hands, good sir."

"What an honour it shall be for you, fragile fellow. Feel free to return the favour in a sparring match." Michael responded, smirking.

"Well Nathan, I expect you know better than to fall for Michael's provoking words. You almost lost a limb the last time." She warned and earned a sour look.

"That was a long time ago, Ai. You do not assume I still am so weak in battle. Why, you have never defeated me in a sparring match." He replied defensively.

Before the princess could retort, a knock on the door caused her to swallow her words. She wondered who it was that needed to see her so early.

"The Lord of the Whall estate." the soldier who opened the door announced. The princess's eyes lit up as the middle-aged man strolled in. Her friends bowed and gave way to the man recognised as one of the greatest nobles in the kingdom.

"Lord Whall," Ai greeted happily.

"Your Highness." The man greeted, giving a graceful bow. He was a fair-haired man with many streaks of grey lining his golden locks. He had a happy countenance and sparkling blue eyes that creased with his smile.

He was the only noble that the princess found amiable. He was somewhat of an uncle to her and treated her with profound kindness and honour. Being one of her father's advisors, he was regularly in the palace and his good nature caused the princess to hope for his presence in any meeting she was made to attend.

"I trust you have been in good health."

"Yes, dear princess. Likewise, I hope." The man said, causing Ai to nod. "Forgive my impertinent morning call, but I must leave to attend to my estate in eastern Ore this morning, and I have with me the list of all who shall attend your ball. I should have left it with your knight, but upon enquiry, I learnt you were awake and present in your library, so here I am."

Ai stared at the scroll in his hand as he put it towards her and frowned. "You do not mean to tell me that you shall be absent from my ball now, do you, sir?"

"No, I shall not miss it for the world. This is why I must hurry to the East and finish my business there, so I shall return in time for the ball." The smile returned to the princess's face as she took hold of the scroll.

"I shall like that very much. It shall be a shame if you are absent."

"You have my word, that I shall ask for the honour to walk you to the ball. But now, I must depart immediately."

"Before you go, sir, please tell me, are there any foreigners on this list?" The royal asked, certain that she would not recognise half of the names on the list.

"Yes, Your Highness, there are some wealthy merchants and nobles from some of the surrounding kingdoms to be present. The king thought to open the invitation to foreign nobles to establish peace. I hope you do not dislike it?"

"No, not at all. On the contrary, I shall like it very much." She said, offering him her hand, which he took and bowed over, before taking his leave.

The princess walked over to her large desk and spread open the long scroll. There were more than a thousand names on the list, most of which the princess did not recognise. She searched in futility for the names of her friends. Although she knew it was not their true names, she hoped she could find a clue that guaranteed their attendance.

"Well, Ai, shall we assume that you know the name of this strange man you met today, and you are searching so committedly to see if he shall attend your ball?" Nathan questioned.

The princess looked up to see that both men were staring curiously at her.

"Of course not, do not be so absurd Nathan. I already told you that I did not know anything about the man. Although now that you have brought it to mind, he might be a foreign merchant, hence his clothes."

"Then we shall have to wonder what he was doing within the palace grounds at such hours," Michael responded.

"There is no winning with you Michael, is there? You might not give me a lecture, but I am quite convinced that I have not heard the last of this."

"Whilst I do not hope to be a bore like our dear Michael, I must own Ai, that it is quite disturbing that a strange man is lurking in the palace gardens. We do not want a repeat of that event we all wish to forget." Nathan said wearily.

"Well, for my part, I did not feel as though I was in danger and you both must own that if the man was indeed after me, he could have hurt me, but he did not. By the by, I am safe and that is that. I do not wish to speak any more of this stranger." The royal said conclusively.

Nathan seemed noncommittal, whilst Michael was insistent on never letting her out of his sight again. The princess could not fault him for this. Since they had never discovered who was responsible for the attack at the orphanage, or if there were more like the thugs who attempted to kill her, he was scrupulous in ensuring her safety.

Ai, however, besides her hopes to see her long-lost friends, also hoped to meet the good stranger, and looked forward to the rest of the festivities in the hope that their paths would once again cross. Her hand reflexively reached out for the drawer on her desk. She pulled out the box where she had carefully kept the letter Sora had given her, and for what seemed to be the thousandth time, she read it to herself.

"My dear Ai,

I am truly saddened that I have been unable to meet with you for the past few days. I, in all truth, wished to no end that I could have met you again, but my circumstances did not allow it.

I proclaim that I cherish the times spent with you in your secret garden, as those remain the most memorable days of my life. I thank you for bringing much joy and gladness to my sister.

On the third day of this very festival, I beheld you seated, in your garden, looking more radiant than the sun which shone upon you. I must confess that I had a strange feeling within me when I saw you. It was one that I could neither comprehend nor did I grudge the unfamiliar sensations in my chest. Even as I write this, I still feel it fresh in my heart at the thought of you.

In all earnest, it is a most enjoyable feeling, and I have never felt this way in all my years on earth. The truth, I must own, is I have felt so since the day I met you, but it has only grown till I am quite unable to control, nor do anything about it.

You are a beautiful jewel, dear Ai, and none compares with you.

I hope above all, and I am quite assured that we shall meet again soon. I regret that I am unable to see you as our hasty departure from your kingdom has only made it possible to write this one letter. I make a solemn promise to forever cherish these feelings, till I see you again.

Yours,

G.

SIX

Ai gazed upon her reflection in the large mirror of her outer chamber and was in awe of the work of her handmaidens. The day of the anniversary of her twenty-first year had finally arrived, and the women at her service exceeded themselves in styling her most suitably for the event. Extravagant twists and curls pinned in an exquisite manner made for a unique hairstyle that only her hair texture could achieve.

All day, she received several gifts from family, nobles, merchants and even commoners. These gifts had been properly scrutinised by her father's men before being handed to her. Her parents spared no expense in lavishing her with the most expensive gifts.

The princess began to believe that her father had successfully given her half of his kingdom by the number of deeds in her name. Her mother gifted her the dress which she was to wear for the ball. It was a violet one embroidered with lace, pearls, and crystals.

As expected, Michael was waiting in front of her chambers with his back turned to her. He turned around as soon as she opened the door, and for a moment, his eyes locked on hers. He looked as though he would have said something, but no words proceeded from his lips. Instead, he stood gazing like he had never set his eyes upon her. At that moment the princess suddenly became conscious of her appearance and was going to ask if he thought she looked odd but was interrupted by Surina.

"Oh, dear me, your highness, you almost forgot your bracelet!" The maiden squeaked from behind her. Ai tore her gaze from her knight and turned to offer her wrist to her handmaiden. She did not think it was of any importance if she did not wear it but did not voice her opinion, since the women had given their all to see her beautifully attired.

"Thank you, Surina." She said as the woman clasped the diamond bracelet around her small wrist. "Now make haste and prepare yourself, so, you are not too late in attending my ball."

"Dearest princess, shall I truly be allowed to attend such an event? I do not think it is proper that I..."

"Away with those excuses, Surina. It is my ball, and I insist on your presence. You must have received my invitation, for I sent it a while ago along with the one for Martha and her husband."

"Yes, I did receive it, but I thought it must have been done in error."

"It was no error, silly girl. You do not think I shall have this celebration without my most trusted maidens present, did you? Now run along and prepare yourself." She declared and turned to Michael, who seemed to have suddenly gained interest in the lamps on the passage. She considered asking him what he thought of her ensemble but decided against it. Instead, she stretched forth her hand to him and watched as he looked at it sceptically.

"What do you mean by this?" He asked with a raised brow.

"Where is it?" Ai questioned.

"Of what do you speak?"

"A gift from you, sir. I searched in futility for it amongst the many I received, but found none in your name,"

"If you received so many gifts, of what significance would one from me be?" He questioned looking amused.

She smiled up at him in response, "I choose to believe that you are yet to comprehend the beauty of receiving presents from dear friends, so I shall speak no further on this matter.

However, I expect you will have learnt this tradition by my next."

As she walked towards the large ballroom, her mind twirled in the hopes of seeing her first friends. She wondered if she would recognise them in the crowds if they did show up.

"My dear princess, how magnificent you look!" Ai looked ahead to see two of the most high-ranked noblemen in Ore awaiting her.

"Lord Whall! I am very pleased to see you. I see you made good your promise to be back in time for the ball." The princess greeted, smiling widely as the man bowed to her.

"Indeed princess, I never go back on my word. The king and queen await you at the ball. Lord Raine and I have their orders to walk you to the entrance of the ball where they await." he explained, gesturing to the other nobleman beside him.

The princess turned to the man, who was in her opinion, the exact opposite of the amiable Lord Whall. He had dark brown hair, with several locks of grey. His forehead was wrinkled with frown lines, and his dark eyes held no joy. He had a strong physique, even though he was middle-aged. Ai had no doubt he had been a dashing young man in his youth since he still had a handsome face, marred only by his ever-stoic countenance.

To her, Lord Raine was the most odious noble in Ore. Other nobles did well to hide their disapproval of her, but the man looked upon her with apparent disdain, as though her very existence was a menace.

"Your Highness," The man greeted with a curt bow.

"Lord Raine," She responded with a nod and a forced smile. He did not return the smile, as his permanent scowl, which was his emblem of disapproval, remained fixed on his ageing face.

"I assure you, sir, the princess is in safe hands. You are dismissed for the rest of the night." Lord Whall said to her knight. Ai turned to Michael, expecting him to rudely disagree as he usually would, but instead, he stepped back and bowed.

"I hope you can attend my ball, Michael." Was all she could say to him before she was led to the entrance of the ballroom where her parents stood waiting. The royal couple took turns embracing, kissing, and praising her before their presence was announced.

They were given a grand welcome with the music playing and the people bowing and curtsying as they sat on the seats prepared for them. Ai nodded absently as her father gave an opening speech about the festivities and its relation to the anniversary of her twenty-first year, all the while distracted in the search for her friends. She saw a few people who bore similar features to them, but none came forward to identify as her friends. After a while, she abandoned the fruitless search and instead focused on searching for the man she ran into in the garden.

King James requested her hand for the first dance, which she willingly obliged, temporarily forgetting her search as she enjoyed dancing with her father, who made her laugh with the silliest jokes. Afterwards, the floor was open to all in attendance. Lord Whall requested a dance with her, and Nathan did after that. After this, the princess had no more dance requests and sat beside her parents.

She was disappointed to see that the ball only had nobles and wealthy merchants in attendance, even though she longed to be acquainted with some commoners. She watched in boredom as people danced and partied, searching in vain for her knight. She noticed her handmaidens present but could tell that Michael was nowhere in the hall, since his huge figure could not be missed. His absence annoyed her more than she expected, as she had wondered if he would request a dance with her.

She suddenly felt the desire to retire for the night, knowing the man would suddenly appear at her side if she left the ball by herself. She was desperate to give him a scold for not attending and realised with a strange feeling of disappointment that the end of the festivities meant that he would not be around her as much. She grimaced at the thought of not having him at her door the next morning.

"I would like to retire to my chambers for the night, Father," she said, with a little yawn. Her father turned to her with a look she could not comprehend in his eyes. "Are you well, father?" she asked, concerned.

"I am very well, dear child. I will however request that you stay till midnight, for I have a final gift to you," The princess looked from him to her mother who was smiling at her and nodding.

"Father, I have received more than enough from you already. I truly do not desire any other gifts, well, except a long healthy life for you and Mother."

"Dearest Ai, you are so precious. However, it is our duty as your parents to give you all our best, so you shall remain till midnight to receive this very present." The queen said, in a conclusive tone that left no room for arguments and the princess resigned herself to several minutes of boredom.

It was a few minutes to midnight when King James signalled for the orchestra to stop, and Ai was ready to receive the said present and be out of the ballroom as soon as it was possible.

"Silence! The King shall address you." Lord Raine yelled to the room, even though there was barely anyone speaking. Ai could not help the irritation she felt at the sound of his voice.

"Here is Ai, my daughter in whom I delight and love. In a short while, the anniversary celebrating the age of her majority shall be over, and I wish to give her a special gift tonight." King James said, his voice reverberating in the hall. Ai felt a feeling of dread wash over her, as her father breathed out heavily, as he did whenever he was worried.

"Hear me people of Ore and dignitaries from far and wide. I have particularly chosen this day to seek an eligible bachelor who desires the hand of the princess of the Ore kingdom in marriage. If you wish to ask for the hand of the princess of Ore, I urge you to come forward, right before midnight."

SEVEN

Ai rose abruptly, her eyes widened in disbelief at Her father's words.

"Father!" She squeaked in dismay but was purposefully ignored. Ai turned to her mother, but Queen Anne was looking straight ahead as if trying her utmost best to avoid her eyes. Ai turned to look at Prophet Asher who had been sitting quietly through the celebration, but he also had his eyes on the people.

She searched in vain for Nathan, but he was nowhere in the room at the time, and she recalled that he had retired early for the night. Her eyes fell back to the King whose gaze was unwavering on the large clock.

"Father, why?" She uttered silently, doing all to withhold the tears that threatened to fall. She felt betrayed, as she had no prior knowledge of her father's intentions.

"Because it is my duty– our duty as your parents to secure your future." The king responded simply.

Ai could not find a suitable response in her mind, so she sat back heavily and waited. As minutes passed by, no one came forward, she thought she was ready to die of embarrassment and rejection but became more concerned about her mother who already had tears flowing down her face.

The painful thought of being undesirable in her kingdom weighed heavy on her mind, but she was convinced that it was a good thing since it meant she would not be given out in marriage to a stranger.

Ai saw her father's shoulder drop and again felt tears welling up in her eyes. She bowed her head, unwilling to show how broken she felt.

Suddenly, the voice of a man echoed through the room. "If your majesty allows it, I will humbly ask for the hand of the princess," The princess abruptly lifted her head, in curious bewilderment. She could not see the man's face as his head was already bowed, but his unique outfit was not one she could recall seeing on anyone in the ballroom. It was an exquisite man's ensemble, with a luxurious robe flung over his shoulders that gave no question of his nobility. She looked around and could see that everyone was just as stunned as she was.

A mixture of various emotions washed over her, causing her to shiver. Whilst she felt relieved that she was not as undesirable as she feared. She was horrified at the prospect of being given out to a man she had never met. She put a hand over her chest, feeling as though she would pass out. Her mother had risen, and a look of relief was apparent in her eyes.

"Raise your head, and state your identity, good sir." the king commanded, and the man obeyed.

Ai gasped in surprise at his face. It was undoubtedly the man from the garden. She could not fathom how he was present in the ballroom when she had intently searched for him earlier. She could see his undeniably handsome features in the well-lit ballroom. He had dark long hair and blue eyes and stood tall with his athletic build and angelic face. Although she had thought about him several times since their last encounter, the last thing she expected was a marriage proposal from him. Several questions without plausible answers plagued her mind.

The man was about to speak up when another man ran and stood beside him and bowed. The man, although dressed as a noble, looked old enough to be her father, with his balding head, long grey beard, and bulging stomach. "Forgive my impertinence, your Majesties and Her Royal Highness, Princess of Ore." He said loudly. "May I present to you, his Royal Majesty, King Johin, of the great kingdom of Bamah." the old man announced, gesturing to the younger man, whilst bowing and stepping out of the way.

Audible gasps and sounds of surprise were heard all over the ballroom and even the king could not hide the look of astonishment on his face. Ai felt her breath hitch in her throat, as she attempted to grasp the entirety of the overwhelming situation.

"You... Ahem..." King James stuttered, before composing himself and speaking up again. "Are you in truth the King of Bamah?" He asked the man.

"Yes, Your Majesty, I am indeed. Accept my apologies for my intrusion into your kingdom, but I could not miss the opportunity, since the festival was open to all," he responded.

"This festival was indeed open to all, so I must say this is no intrusion in my kingdom. However, this ball was not, and I shall ask how you gained entry in the future, but first, I must ask, if this means that King Bethenel is dead,"

"Yes, Your Majesty, he and my mother the queen expired at sea in a shipwreck last year, and I have only been crowned King for about a year now," The man responded calmly.

"Pray tell, for it remains beyond my comprehension, why do you, the king of the strongest kingdom seek my daughter's hand?" King James questioned, and it was evident to Ai that he was suspicious of the man, and did not believe he was who he claimed to be.

"You can trust, Your Majesty, that I have no hidden intentions. The princess and I are acquainted, and this is by no means my first encounter with her. I do not doubt that she's the one I wish to wed as she has no rival in my heart." The Bamish king declared so confidently that Ai was tempted to believe him.

King James raised an eyebrow, "Not your first encounter? I see." The princess who was still too stunned to speak, shrank in embarrassment at her father's amused look. She had not told her father that she had run into the strange man and wondered what obscure thoughts were going through his mind. She hoped he did not think she had again begun some clandestine meetings against his clear instructions. She waited in vain for the man to say he was jesting and was the simple commoner she had met in the garden.

"Dear sir, you will agree that it is quite obligatory that I request proof of your claim, as words alone do not suffice." King James said.

"Of course, I should not be so foolish as to have nothing to back my claim. I have with me my signet ring and my seal of honour. If those two do not suffice, permit me to show you the sword of the sovereign of Bamah." The man said, brushing off the robe that hid the sword at his side. The palace guards immediately took defensive positions.

Since weapons had been prohibited in the palace, there was a question of how he not only gained access, along with his man but got in with a weapon. King James raised his hand signalling for the guards to be at ease.

"Forgive me for bringing a weapon, but I knew for certain it was the only way I could prove my status without a doubt," he said, presenting his sword to a soldier, who took it to the King.

King James took the sword and observed the precious stones on the hilt as well as the inscription on the double-edged sword and nodded.

"This is indeed the sword of the king of Bamah. You are wise to have brought it, since it was created here in Ore, using our precious stones. A unique sword was gifted to each sovereign present at the first Yachad festival." He expressed, staring at the weapon reminiscently. "I shall acknowledge you as a king but will keep you at arm's length till all is confirmed without a shadow of a doubt. As for my daughter's hand in marriage..." Before he could complete his words, Ai picked up her skirt and ran out of the ballroom through a back door.

She vaguely heard her parents call out after her but was too angry and embarrassed to heed their voices. No palace guard dared to stop or question her. She knew running to her secret place would do little good, but it provided a window of escape for her, even for a few moments. She hoped to recollect her thoughts before she was obliged to stand before her father again.

She went through the hidden door, and sat heavily on a bench, glad to be away from the suffocating ballroom and grateful for the full moonlight that illuminated the garden. She caught her breath and realised that anger dominated her tumultuous emotions.

She was angry at her father who decided to give her out in marriage without her knowledge or prior consent, and at her mother who was an apparent accomplice. Most of her anger, however, was directed at the Bamish king.

Just as Michael had warned, he was most assuredly a suspicious figure. Even if he was indeed the King of the most powerful kingdom, she would have to wonder at his motives for proposing marriage to her after one meeting.

It was no hidden fact that the reason for the abrupt end of the Yachad Festival was that the then-Bamish King had sought an alliance that would allow his kingdom to dominate the others.

King Bethenel had chosen no allegiance when the other kingdoms refused to submit to his proposal since Bamah possessed vast resources and did not necessarily need trade relations with any other kingdom.

His actions had brought an end to the Yachad festival, and Ai had secretly despised him for it. She reasoned that the proposed marriage was a ploy of the present Bamish king to dominate and eventually conquer her kingdom.

After several minutes of pondering on various ploys of Bamah, Ai felt her nerves begin to calm as the cold summer night wind hit her skin. She became increasingly concerned about her lack of warm clothing. She shivered as she wrapped her arms around her small person. Royal balls usually ended hours past midnight, but she was certain if she waited, she could quietly return to her chambers and avoid an interview with her parents.

That is if I am not expired in this wind by then.

The sound of footsteps at the hidden door of the garden put her thinking to an abrupt end. She arose, hoping it was Nathan or Michael, but the possibility that it was her father, was worrying to her. She did not expect him to visit her garden on such an occasion, since the secret could be compromised if he did.

To her ultimate bewilderment, the most unexpected visitor graced her secret place, and she stood stunned and unable to speak as the moonlight shone upon the handsome man.

"How...? When? What...? Where are the...?" The princess stuttered, unable to think up the right question to ask the intruder.

"Forgive me, Ai. I must have startled you, that was not my intention," he said softly.

The princess looked at him incredulously, more surprised at the casual and informal way he spoke to her.

"Pray tell, sir, what exactly are your intentions? And more importantly, how in heaven's name did you find this place."

"It is just as I said earlier, it was not my…"

"You deceived me, pretending to be a common man of this land," she interrupted, unable to hold back her annoyance.

"It was never my intention to pretend or deceive you. We met in such unexpected circumstances, that I thought it would be unwise to reveal my identity at that moment," he responded.

"Well sir, what are your true intents? If you are indeed king, this must be some sort of petty attempt to take over my kingdom, but I can assure you, that I shan't let it happen."

"That is not the case. You have my word that I do not care for your kingdom. I care for you." The man said, taking bold strides towards her.

Ai, determined not to back down or show fear, stood firm, and stared up at him as he approached her. "Your word has no weight with me, sir, for I neither know who you are, nor what your true intentions are. I shall very well like to know how you located this place and why you are here." She said warily, as he closed the distance between them.

"Never mind that Ai, the more important question is, why on earth are you trying to freeze yourself to death?" He asked, taking off his robe and putting it over her shoulders. As much as she desired to take off the warm, furry robe and throw it in his face, she could not bring herself to, as she was shivering visibly from the cold.

"What do you want from me?" she questioned in defeat, as the impropriety of their being alone in a garden was beginning to dawn on her and she wished dearly to be in her chambers.

"I desire to wed you, Ai." The response and the tenderness she saw in his eyes which shone in the moonlight, unnerved her.

"And why would you desire that?" she questioned taking several backward strides away from the man, who was becoming more and more unscrupulous in her sight.

"Because I am utterly besotted with you."

The princess gazed at him through gaping eyes, taken aback by his incredible words. "Pray, tell, sir, how could it be? We have met only that one time, and it is not sufficient for you to be considered an acquaintance. I shall not be deceived by such cunning falsity." She had become certain that it was a deceitful plot, and the man probably thought her gullible, because of the rejection he had witnessed her experience.

"No, no, my dear Ai, this is no plot or anything of that sort. You must believe that my words are true. I have felt this way for so many years, long before I knew what the feelings meant."

The princess frowned at his words, as she attempted to make sense of it. "What do you mean by this, sir?" she asked weakly, as the possibilities of his meaning hit her like a storm. The words from the letter she received all those many years ago, came afresh to her.

"Surely, you must know what I mean, Ai. You, my dear, were my first true friend and I have not met any quite like you. In the short time we spent together as children, I became so fond of you and did not realise how much, till we were separated. I shall confess that no one on earth has stirred up the emotions you have, and I knew that there was no one else I would rather spend the rest of my life with."

Ai opened her mouth to speak, but no words proceeded. She put her hand over her heart, in a vain attempt to bring cohesion to her tumultuous mind, as the words he spoke left no room for doubt.

He was her dear friend, *Sora*.

EIGHT

Ai gazed up at the man who was looking at her with a patient smile. He indeed possessed similar features to the friend she had long been separated from. She had been unable to spot his distinguishing features the first time they met in the garden, and when he had come forward at the ball, she had not been in the right frame of mind to consider the possibilities. He had grown to possess such manly attributes that the young boy she knew could hardly be seen in him.

The princess took some staggering steps backwards, overwhelmed with the entirety of their circumstance. She was about to speak, when suddenly, in what seemed like a flash, a most familiar sturdy figure blocked her vision. Michael stood with his back to her, and a sword pointed at the Bamish king. As usual, she was confounded by the speed and quietness with which he appeared. It had been odd that he had not been at her side as soon as she stepped out.

"Princess! Are you hurt?" he asked rather desperately, as he turned to her, his eyes going over her person with evident apprehension.

At that moment, she was reminded of the time he had appeared at the orphanage and risked his life for hers. It was apparent that he had seen her stagger and had assumed the worst of the foreign king. She wanted to explain to him that this was different and that this man meant her no harm but struggled to get words out of her dishevelled mind. She could only watch as the bold king continued to approach her, ignoring the threatening weapon pointed at him. He did not appear to be intimidated by the soldier as he was not much shorter and possessed a sturdy build too. He stepped out of the way of the sword and continued to walk towards her, and she noticed the knight was about to strike.

"Michael! Stand down at once!" Ai yelled out with urgency truly afraid he would hurt her friend. The soldier turned to her with apparent confusion, but she turned her eyes to the young king before her.

"Sora?" She questioned, her words fading in her throat.

"Yes Ai, it is I." The man responded. "My true name is Johin, and I am now King over my kingdom."

"How... Why...?" Ai stuttered as words eluded her.

"I shall explain it to you shortly, but we must return to the ballroom at once, as I have been given an ultimatum. I make a solemn vow that I shall not compel you to wed me against your wish, for I desire to win your heart. However, I shall surely lose the chance to do so, if you do not go back with me to your father." he said desperately.

"No! I must ascertain that you are indeed Sora. Tell me two things which you alone would know."

"Whilst my knowledge of this garden should be proof enough, I shall leave you without a shadow of a doubt." The man said and smiled down upon her. "The first is that I have a sister who you fondly called Hana. The second is, that I sent a letter to you on the last day of the Yachad festival. I recall the words I wrote, which hold my dearest regard for you. It is the one way I have beheld you in my thoughts since we were separated." he said and took her hand in his. Ai was compelled to look into his eyes as he whispered the words, "You are my beautiful jewel, and none compares with you."

The princess felt her breath cease for a moment. The man before her was undoubtedly the boy she met at the Yachad festival, but she did not know how she felt about reuniting, over a marriage proposal.

"If you will, dear Ai, I must take you back to your father, lest he denies me the chance to ask for your hand." Ai simply nodded, deciding that she could make decisions the next day. He took her hand, ready to leave the garden, only to find their path was obstructed by her knight. His sword was sheathed, and his face revealed no emotions, but the princess was too embarrassed to look in his eyes, as she recalled how curtly she had ordered him to step down.

"Please Michael, I believe I can trust him." She said quietly, resisting the king's pull to go past him. It was evident that he did not care for her knight's opinion, but she did. Michael raised a brow at her but moved out of their way and followed right behind them. She hoped he had caught on to the circumstance as he usually did, and he could tell that the king was an old friend and not a stranger to her.

As they walked, Ai tried bringing cohesion to her chaotic reflections, and by the time she had successfully put her mind in order, they were already standing at the doors of the grand hall.

The awkwardness of returning to the hall on the arm of a foreign King mortified her as much as the inevitably dreadful reactions of her parents. She retracted her hand abruptly as the doors flung open, and every eye was upon them.

"Well, if this is not the most shocking thing, I have had to behold in all my years!" Her father said, looking amused as they approached him. He turned from her to the Bamish king, "Dear sir, you have been undeniably successful in the quest placed before you and since I gave my word, I shall not deny your advances. It is rather late tonight, and the princess disclosed to me earlier that she is weary, so, I shall permit her to retire to her chambers. We shall meet in my throne room at noon tomorrow, to further discuss this."

Ai did not waste a breath after he spoke. She curtsied to her parents and hurried out of the hall, followed by her handmaidens. As soon as they arrived at her chambers and the door was shut, she turned to Surina, who looked ready to burst with excitement. Martha stood solemnly and said nothing.

"Well, Surina, out with it," Ai said, giggling at the look on the younger maiden's face.

"Oh, dear princess, I have so many questions. I feel so excited that I might faint."

"Do well to help the princess undress before you do, dear girl," Martha said strictly.

"Please Martha, do not be so cold, for I also am overwhelmed with emotions," Ai commented and turned again to the excited handmaiden. "I collect that you seek to understand how I came to return with the foreign king." Surina nodded eagerly like a puppy, causing Ai to laugh again. "I must, however, suffer you, to first narrate how it was that he came to seek me out."

This did not in any way disappoint Surina, as she looked even more excited to tell the tale. She slowly narrated how King James had made a move to go after the princess when she ran off, but King Johin "graciously" stepped up and requested to go after her. King James refused at first, stating that he would bring the ball to a close and attend to his daughter.

"Please your Majesty, all I ask is this one chance to bring her back to you and then you may give me leave to seek her hand," Surina said in a deep voice, attempting to mimic the Bamish king. It made Ai laugh and she was glad that she had insisted on her handmaiden's attendance at the ball.

"His Majesty proclaimed that he was certain the king of Bamah would never find you but gave him the chance to seek you and bring you back to the ballroom before it was half past midnight. I can assure you, dear princess, that it was most shocking that you returned with him. I do not doubt that everyone at the ball was amazed that he had found you and convinced you in such a short time. I am most eager to know what induced you to follow that strange, but handsome man."

"My dear Surina, he is assuredly not a strange man, but a friend I met at the Yachad festival. Martha would know his identity, as she was my handmaiden at the time." This declaration caused the silent woman to gasp.

"Surely, you do not mean to say, he is that young royal boy that played along with you and his sister in your garden.

"Yes, dear Martha, it is he."

"Oh, of everything so romantic!" Surina professed, twirling around the chambers. "Reunited with a long-lost love."

"Stop your dallying, lest you knock some candles over! If you have nothing better to do, help the princess remove her accessories." Martha scolded, and although the younger maiden did stop twirling, she was not put out of countenance, as she took the princess's hands.

"How is it that you never spoke of him, and you were always teasing poor Martha on falling in love..."

"Oh, stop Surina, it is nothing of that sort." The princess replied laughing at the animated way her handmaiden was acting. She was in truth calmed by her reactions and allowed herself to laugh off her worries.

"Surely it must be love. Why else shall a king leave his kingdom to request your hand? And why should you agree, if he was not your beloved?"

"Again Surina, it is not as you have imagined. I had only seen twelve summers in this world when I met the man. There was no thought of romantic love in my head at the time. Whatever reason he has offered for me is just as strange to me as it is to you."

The handmaiden ceased pressing the matter and shifted her focus to the people's reactions when they heard that such an important person had offered for the princess. Her words, as she abused the people for not offering before the foreign king did, put a damper on Ai's spirits, as she was again put in mind of the rejection she had faced. She was embarrassed that Sora had also had to witness how unpopular she was in her kingdom.

By the next morning, she was able to successfully collect her thoughts and decided that she needed to stop acting like a shy little girl, and like a princess who had just attained her majority. It was with this determination that she received her handmaidens, and since they appeared to have noticed that she had suddenly been put out of countenance the previous night, they were happy about her change of disposition.

Breakfast was brought to her chambers, and she sat with Surina, listening to her tell all that she had heard of the Bamish king in the past and present.

"A most beautiful creature, do you not think, dear princess? At least that is what every woman seems to call him. He is almost as beautiful as your gallant knight– Well, except that he is perhaps, less athletic. Nonetheless, he is not a mere knight, but one of the most powerful sovereigns on earth, and that makes him so perfect." The handmaiden expressed freely, and Ai listened absently as she considered how she could go about her day. She arose suddenly, interrupting Surina from whatever praises she was ascribing to the king of Bamah.

"Your Highness?" Surina questioned, looking confused.

"I must go to my father at once."

"But, Your Highness, the King requested your presence at noon."

"Yes, yes, Surina, but I wish to speak to him before everyone else gathers. My father shall not refuse me."

Ai was not too surprised to see Michael waiting outside her chambers, but all her will to be a dignified princess left her as she felt like shrinking in embarrassment when he gazed upon her.

She had spent a good part of the night rueing how she had addressed him and ignored him after Johin had taken her hand and led her back to the ballroom.

Although Johin had been her first friend, it had only been for a few days in the past. Michael on the other hand had been beside her, almost every day of her life since her fifteenth year. She could not help the feeling of disloyalty that she felt as she slowly lifted her eyes to the overly loyal knight.

"Ahem... uh... The King..." he stuttered, and for the first time since she had known him, she noticed uncertainty in his eyes. It was however gone almost as soon as she noticed it. He cleared his throat and spoke again. "I am here on the king's order. He has asked me to remain at your side since the circumstances have changed."

Ai stared at him for a moment, debating within herself if it was necessary to offer an explanation and apology for how harsh she was at the garden.

"Michael–" She began.

"I shall do all to be out of your way in your dealings with the supposed king, so do not let my presence worry you." He said, evidently misunderstanding her disposition.

NINE

Ai did all to push the feelings of disloyalty out of her mind, arguing within herself that she was a princess, and did not owe the knight her loyalty.

However, after walking a few steps towards the throne room, she was certain that it would only depress her further to remain silent. She halted and turned to Michael, who had been following behind her. He raised a brow, as he was forced to stop abruptly.

"Princess?"

"Sir!" She exclaimed, feeling unnerved, but determined. "I must explain the circumstances of last night!"

"You owe me no such explanation." He replied monotonously, causing the princess to frown.

"Michael, if this is one of your boring fits of being a dignified knight, please put it away, for it is the most disagreeable thing about you. I am aware that many believe it makes you appear gallant, but I assure you, dear sir, that it is nothing of that sort." She said in such a burst of annoyance that she almost forgot her purpose for addressing him, but it soon returned to her mind, and she put a hand over her mouth.

"Oh, dear Michael, forgive me, how odious I must sound. I did hope to beg your pardon for being so unkind to you last night in my garden. But what must you do, except provoke me into saying quite the opposite of what I intended."

The knight's straight face broke into an amused smile. "I must confess that I find it quite diverting to have you speak in such a comical manner, but to blame me for it is beyond anything I have heard."

"But you know you are to blame. Yes, sir, I am convinced that you do, for you are a most calculating and intelligent man. You alone know how to put me out of all sorts in a moment, even when I am in the best humour."

"I must say you give me too much credit than I deserve, Your Highness, but I shall relent and beg your pardon for being so odiously calculating, intelligent and worse, provoking." He said with quivering lips.

"I can see that you are laughing at me, and I am glad to be a source of amusement to you. Oh, what an annoying man you are!" She said, folding her arms and turning from him.

"Forgive me, princess." He said calmly. "What must I do to not be so, provoking?"

At these words, she turned to him with a hopeful look and smiled. "Well, shall I tell you how I came to be in that situation yesterday?"

"In truth, I do not think it is of any consequence that you explain it, but lest I provoke you to rain down fire and brimstone upon my person, I shall hear every detail you wish to disclose."

Ai frowned at this, unsure if to be annoyed at the first or middle part of his statement. She was mollified at his willingness to listen and decided to ignore everything else he said. "Shall we go to my library then?" She asked and began to walk in the opposite direction of her initial destination, giving the knight no chance to object.

As soon as they arrived at the room, the princess began to tell him how she came to meet her friends at the Yachad festival. She purposefully omitted the circumstance that had compelled her to run from the room filled with royals and collide with the boy who became her first friend. She told him of her wonderful experience with Hana and Sora, up to the point of receiving the letter on the very last day.

The knight listened intently, but Ai could not tell what he was thinking from his emotionless face. He was leaning against the library door with his arms folded. She looked up at him curiously as she finished her tale.

"I do hope, Michael, that you understand why I was obliged to follow him. I would not have done so if I had only met him in the garden a few days ago. Also, I thought you were about to kill him, and it was on that account, I spoke so harshly, and I beg your pardon for that. I was still in a daze, so I was unable to explain anything to you at that moment."

"Nor should you have felt any need to…"

"Michael, on my word, if you say anything to provoke me into fits…"

"I shall not, I assure you. What I meant to say is that it was quite apparent that he was not unfamiliar to you. I do believe that you have more wit than to trust a person you have only just met. I hope dearly that you do not think me so dim-witted to kill any person without good reason, especially one who claims to be the king of such a powerful kingdom. I made a vow, after the orphanage incident, to do all to avoid killing anyone, especially in your presence. I heard from Nathan that you had many sleepless nights after that day."

"Well, I am much obliged to you, for I am sadly most squeamish and cannot stand the sight of blood or a lifeless person. I must confess that I did perceive that you thought I was in danger and would have done all to save me, even if it meant murdering a king." She said laughing.

"Well, you thought wrong. I did hope to scare him or at worst, impale him in no fatal way."

The princess scrunched up her face at the thought of Michael hurting her friend. "In that case, I am glad I stopped you. How did you come to find me?"

"Surely you must know that I would never let you wonder around the palace by yourself. I was with you from the time you stepped out of the ball. I am certain it is the only reason the king allowed that man wander freely. I would have stopped him as soon as he entered your garden, but I could tell he was permitted to seek you out."

"But Michael, you must admit that he is very bold. He did not shudder at the sight of your weapon, instead, he kept advancing fearlessly."

"Yes, I can admit that he is quite courageous, but you must forgive me, for I cannot share the trust you have in him. In truth, I am increasingly distressed by his continued presence in Ore. From all you have told me, there is nothing that proves he is the King of Bamah. I shall therefore keep watch to ensure you do not come to harm." The knight said conclusively.

Ai sighed, knowing it would be quite useless to argue with him. "Do whatever makes you feel knightly, Michael." She muttered sardonically. "Now, I must hurry to my father before the meeting at noon. It was where I was headed before you had me utterly diverted."

"That, princess, is most unjust, for I recall telling you how unnecessary an explanation was, but gave in to your insistence, so as not to appear so 'gallant' or 'provoking.'"

"I must tell you, that you appear vainglorious, regardless of what you do. Come now, let us hurry to my father, for I know it will be futile to ask you not to follow me. Especially now when you have become so suspicious of my dear friend."

Michael smiled and opened the door to her. She was hopeful to speak to her father about the ball and to make him promise to refrain from making any such mortifying pronouncements in the future.

She arrived at the doors of the throne room and the palace guards bowed to her. One of the soldiers was asking if she would like to be announced when her father's angry voice reverberated through the walls. Ai stood still, ignoring the soldier's question.

"How dare they do that to their princess?"

"Princess?" She heard Michael's wary voice from behind her, but she ignored it. As unbecoming as eavesdropping was, the chances her father would tell her of the situation that made him so cross were slim, so she hoped to hear it without his knowledge.

"Be calm now, James." Her mother's soft voice was heard next, with much difficulty.

"But the horrendous lies they spread about her! Why should anyone sabotage her chances to be wed? I am most certain that these rumours were started by a nobleman. They were the only ones I told of my intentions before the ball." Her father thundered.

"Are you certain of these rumours, sir?" her mother asked and a voice she instantly recognised answered.

"Yes, Your Majesty, without a doubt. My wife told me of it this morning on my return to my estate from the ball. It was the reason she forbade my son from attending. I had no idea of it, as I only returned to Belleich in time for the ball. I was quite upset to see that my family, or at least my son, was not in attendance, for my wife is always sickly. Had I known of this absurd scheme, I would have reported it immediately. Whoever began the rumours must have ensured every noble and wealthy person in attendance heard of it, so that none would propose to the princess." Lord Whall explained.

The princess did her all to calm her stormy emotions. One thing was certain, someone or a group of people were working relentlessly towards her detriment, and she was determined to get to the bottom of it.

TEN

Ai walked into the throne room, after permitting a soldier to announce her presence. She was hopeful she could hide how affected she was by what she had heard earlier. Michael remained outside the doors, as she was undoubtedly safe with the king.

"Father, mother," She greeted, curtsying, and observing the apprehensive look they both tried to hide.

"Oh, dear child, you are here early," Her mother said.

"Yes mother, I wished to speak to father before the arranged time."

"Your Highness," Lord Whall greeted with a bow, and Ai turned to him with a sweet smile. She felt obliged to him for his disclosure. He was indeed the only nobleman she could trust and rely on.

"Dear Lord Whall, how do you do?"

Her father cleared his throat and spoke with a forced smile. "My dear child, what is it you wish to speak to me about? Do you require a private audience?"

"No Father, I believe I can speak freely as it is. I simply wish to express how bewildered I was by your pronouncement yesterday. You neither sought my opinion nor approval on the matter." Ai queried.

"My dear girl, I did wonder how long it would take you to express displeasure over my unexpected, but well-meant actions. It did not take too long." He said and laughed. "As always, I am well prepared to suffer the consequences. Now, ask me anything to the half of my kingdom and it shall be yours."

"Oh, father! You already know what my answer is to that." Ai said, sighing in defeat. She was convinced that her father had been prepared for her reaction beforehand.

The princess was about to speak again when a soldier announced the presence of Lord Raine. He entered looking as dignified as he usually did. Despite her dislike for him, the princess could not deny how majestic he was in person. He greeted her parents with a graceful bow and offered her his usual curt bow.

Ai observed him with suspicion and was almost certain he was responsible for the rumours. A moment after his entrance, Prophet Asher entered the throne room alongside Nathan. By the sound of the church bell, she was aware that it was noon, and their meeting was about to commence.

The king of Bamah arrived with five men following and for the first time, the princess was able to behold him in the fullness of the daylight. His eyes were as blue as she remembered, his straight dark hair was tied neatly behind him, and his comely face was even more beautiful than she had beheld in the shadows. He was dressed in royal apparel and appeared so gallant that the princess found it quite difficult to pull her gaze from him. After offering greetings to her parents, he turned to her with a smile and bowed gracefully. But she turned away, too flustered to observe him any further.

She looked at the empty seat on the left side of the king's throne and sighed. It was a chair on which she usually sat whenever she was privileged to witness her father judge the cases brought to him. She never imagined that she would be on the receiving end of the room.

She looked around the room, glad to see that no other nobles were present and wished Lord Raine would be immediately removed. Her eyes rested on Nathan and noticed a cheesy grin plastered on his face. She sighed, assured that she would be taunted to no end as soon as he had the chance.

"Tell me, my dear child, how is it that you accepted the proposal of a man who you have only just met?" King James questioned pulling her gaze to himself.

"But I have not just met him, father…"

"Yes, yes, I assumed you met during this festival, but what I cannot fathom, is how it is that he came to find you and convince you to return with him in such a short time. From your reaction at the ball, you appeared rather displeased with his proposal, so tell me, why did you eventually accept?" the king asked, doing little to hide his amusement.

"It is quite true father that I met him in the course of the festival, but that, I assure you, was not the first time I met him. We first became acquainted as children, several years ago." She responded and was satisfied with the surprised looks she received from her audience.

"Could you have met him during one of your escapades to that orphanage?" The queen questioned with a hint of amusement in her voice.

"No Mother, we came to be friends during the first Yachad festival," Ai responded rapidly, nettled by her mother's choice of words.

"Ai, despite this informal meeting, we do believe you are capable of making wise decisions. We are neither trying to approve nor disapprove of your choice. We simply wished to ascertain why you made that choice." King James expressed and nodded at the Prophet, who stood and spoke.

"I shall now address you, children. The purpose of this meeting is to let you know that you have our blessing to court each other and decide if you truly wish to be married. However, you shall also require our blessing to wed if it does come to that. It may appear shocking to you, Your Majesty of the Bamish kingdom, that I, a Prophet, speak these words. I must tell you that, in Ore, we put the Almighty God and His words above all, and being the Prophet, my words are honoured as well. I do hope you understand that I mean you no offence."

"I take no offence, good sir," Johin replied.

"Dear Ai, now that you have our blessings to court, you must do it within the confines of the palace rules." Her father said to her and turned to address the foreign king. "I have been meaning to ask you, sir, how was it that you were able to bring a weapon into the palace? I can understand how you were able to attend the festival, but it should have been impossible to gain entrance to the palace with a weapon, especially one the size of your sword."

"You see, I am quite skilled, Your Majesty, and slipping past your soldiers was no bigger than child's play." He said, giving nothing away.

Although her father said nothing for a moment, Ai could tell from the creases on his forehead that he was disturbed by this revelation and foresaw a storm of questions brewing in his mind. She intervened quickly before her father turned the interview into an interrogation.

"May we be excused, father," she asked, causing the king to raise his brows at her. After what felt like an age, he nodded, and she turned to her royal friend. "Would you accompany me to my library?" She asked and the young king obliged, allowing her to lead him out of the throne room.

The princess was surprised that Michael was nowhere in sight but was gladdened, as she did not wish to feel the weight of the awkwardness from the previous night. As soon as they were in the quietness of her library, Ai ensured the door was left slightly ajar for propriety reasons.

"King..."

"Please princess, call me Johin." He interrupted before she had the opportunity to speak further.

"Johin, how is my dear friend Hana?"

"She is in good health. She never ceases speaking so fondly of you."

"I too have thought of her every waking day and hoped to see her in this festival."

"Just her?" Johin questioned with a smirk.

"In truth, I did hope to see you both, but I am quite disappointed that Hana is not here." The princess expressed. "May I ask why you decided to journey all this way to my kingdom?"

"I thought it was my sole chance to see you again. News reached me that Ore was opening its gates for a festival, and I knew that nothing on earth could stop me from attending. You see, my sister and I have sought an opportunity to see you again for quite some time, but our kingdoms were not particularly on friendly terms."

"How did you know I would be in the garden on the morning I ran into you?" Ai asked, eager to have all her questions answered.

"That was pure coincidence, I assure you, but a most pleasant one. I stood there reminiscing on the old days and was considering visiting your garden when you collided with me." He responded smiling.

"I beg your pardon. It was a most embarrassing encounter."

"I am delighted it occurred, for I was gifted the opportunity of seeing your beautiful face at the rise of the sun." He took hold of her hands, compelling her to look up into his blue eyes. "I have been captivated by you since I could comprehend what my feelings meant. Seeing you again only made me realise how much I want to be with you and no one else." He declared boldly.

ELEVEN

The princess stood dazed by the genuineness in his eyes. She was uncertain that she could reciprocate his feelings at that moment, but she revelled in being accepted by him without prejudice.

"Ahem!" She heard a most familiar voice cough, and she abruptly pulled away from the king. She should have been aware that Michael would be lurking somewhere around her. Being the overprotective knight he was, it was unusual that she hadn't seen him since they stepped out of the throne room. She could however not deny that he was a welcome interruption as she did not know how to respond to Johin.

"Forgive my impertinence, but I am certain it would annoy the princess to no end if I were a silent witness to such an impassioned moment, so I chose to make my presence known. Now, you may freely continue, do not mind me." The knight was leaning against a book rack with folded arms.

She felt lightheaded at the thought of whatever he had assumed was about to happen, but there was no less awkward way to convince him that he was certainly thinking wrongly, especially if he had witnessed their conversation.

"I do not know if ever I shall get used to your antics, Michael, but you almost scared the ghost out of me!" she exclaimed in a bid to overcome the awkwardness of the situation.

"I wish to have a private moment with the princess." King Johin said in a firm tone. Ai recognised the irritation in his voice and was not surprised at this, since his first encounter with Michael was with a sword to his throat. He was unaware of Michael's duty as her knight and there was no doubt he seemed like a nuisance.

"I'm sure you do, but it is most unfortunate that I cannot grant it," Michael responded, standing straight, and stepping forward, as though to show the small but significant height difference between himself and the king. "You see, you have given us nothing, but a sword, your name and a few unknown men to attest to your identity. We could never be certain that the sword was not stolen, and your men are not bandits dressed in robes with evil intentions towards the princess. I must be here to snap your neck the moment I sense that is the case." He said in such a convincing tone that could have caused any ordinary person to quiver in fear. The foreign king however stood frowning. Ai, familiar with Michael's tactics, stepped between the men and gave the knight a warning stare.

"Impostor or not, you shall do no such thing, Michael." She knew he was only trying to intimidate the king, but she could see that it was making Johin furious. "Do not jest about such a thing, for it fills my head with repugnant images I prefer not to behold."

"Yes, yes, Your Highness, I shall not kill," Michael responded, with amusement in his voice. "I cannot however be easily rid of, especially when I perceive that you might be in danger. Besides, princess, you must realise the impropriety of being with any man, especially an unknown stranger, unchaperoned."

Ai glared at him and turned to Johin, whose face was red with apparent annoyance. "Pardon my knight, King Johin, he is overprotective and irks me to no end since he was ordered by my father to guard me so closely. But I assure you he is one I can trust with my life," she explained. "Shall we go into the garden, where Michael can watch from afar, but not listen in on our conversations?" She asked with a smile, hoping to break the tension.

"It would be my pleasure," Johin responded, his expression softening as he shifted his gaze to her. He offered his hand, and Ai stared at it for a moment, conscious of the fact that her knight's watchful eyes were on them.

She was about to put her hand into his, when hasty footsteps were heard approaching, and suddenly Nathan stood in the doorway. She was quick to withdraw her hand, unwilling to subject herself to any teasing remarks from her friend.

"Ai, father has sent for you." He said, carelessly, almost ignoring the foreign king. Ai did not miss the look of astonishment on Johin's face. She was certain that he was surprised at the informal manner Nathan addressed her, but she had little will to explain their relationship.

"Forgive me Johin, but I must go. The Prophet seeks me, and I do not doubt the urgency," she explained, offering him an apologetic look.

"Shall I get a guard to walk you to your assigned chambers, sir?" Michael asked, and Ai nodded in agreement.

"That will not be necessary," Johin responded curtly. His frown returned and Ai could tell he was not pleased.

"As you wish." Michael replied, giving him a smug look.

Johin turned to her with a raised brow, as though willing her to speak against Michael, but the princess did not utter a word. After a strenuous night thinking about how she addressed him in the garden, she was unwilling to say any harsh words to him ever again. She instead muttered her apologies to the king and hurriedly followed her friend out of her library.

Nathan quietly led her to his father and left as soon as she got to the office, but she knew better than to expect that he would leave the matter of her courtship alone. She was certain that his honour for his father was the only thing that made him contain whatever words he wished to amuse himself with.

Michael, however, did not leave her side, and she was grateful for this, as she did not wish to have any more awkward moments with Johin, nor did she wish to respond to his feelings at any immediate date.

By noon the next day, after a round of amusing chatter from her younger handmaiden, she stepped out of her chambers to see her knight awaiting. Whilst they had been cordial after the long meeting with the prophet the previous day, she could not help the feeling of embarrassment, that was invoked by the memory of his witnessing the conversation between herself and the Bamish king.

She was most thankful, when he did not say anything about the past events as they walked towards her library. It was very much in his character, and it was only in such circumstances, that she was thankful for his gallant nature.

Nathan would never show as much grace. She thought, and as though conjured, the friend in question came up from around a corner. As soon as the princess caught sight of him, she turned around, almost colliding with Michael in her bid to get away. The knight had his hands on her shoulders, stopping her from crashing into his broad chest. He gave her a questioning look, but understanding replaced confusion as he looked beyond her, and smiled knowingly.

"Now, now, Ai, do not try to escape me," Nathan called, running up towards them. The princess turned around knowing there was no hope of avoiding her friend.

"Nathan, before you begin your endless teasing remarks, intending to embarrass me for no good cause, I challenge you to a mock duel. If I win, you shall never speak anything about the events of these past few days. If you do win, you can have your fill taunting me to no end." She watched Michael and Nathan mirror looks of amusement and the latter broke into a fit of laughter.

"Ti's quite brave of you to think you can defeat me in a duel when you have failed to win a single sparring match against me," he replied, shaking his head.

After the orphanage incident, and her father engaged an Ore soldier to train her in swordsmanship, she began sparring with Nathan in her free time and bore several losses. Although she had begged to spar with Michael, he had only indulged her once. The one time she could never forget...

"It is different now, for losing comes at a cost. I must defend whatever is left of my honour." Ai said, causing both men to laugh again.

"You can laugh now, but you shan't be laughing when I win." She insisted, with a look of determination.

Before Nathan had a chance to respond, some soldiers marched hurriedly past them. They paused and bowed to the princess before continuing.

"Halt!" Ai commanded, and the men obeyed. "What is the cause of the commotion?" She questioned, as it was obvious that there was something unusual happening. One of the men stepped forward and answered.

"Your Highness, there are soldiers at the Northern borders claiming to be from the kingdom of Bamah and are here for their king. We are making haste to ensure security in the palace."

"Is my father aware of this?" She asked, and the man confirmed that he was, so she dismissed them to go about their duties.

"So, he truly is the Bamish king," Nathan stated dryly.

"Did you doubt it?" Ai questioned, incredulously.

"I did indeed, and do not look at me so, for I am quite certain Michael shared my sentiments," Nathan responded.

"It would be unwise to trust a man simply because he presents a sword, princess," Michael corroborated, nonchalantly.

"I am not surprised at your words, Michael, for your actions speak even louder," Ai said, shaking her head, as she recalled how he treated the foreign king the previous day. "Come now, let us go and see how father handles the matter. I imagine he might share your sentiments."

TWELVE

Ai sat beside her parents in the throne room as King Johin walked in, followed by the five who had been with him the previous day. There were several nobles gathered there, including Lord Whall and Lord Raine.

"Well, King Johin, may I assume that you know the reason why we have gathered and requested your presence?"

"I believe so, Your Majesty. News has just reached me that an army from my kingdom is at your borders. May I assure you that they mean your kingdom no harm but have only come to seek me."

"I assume they would know better than to foolishly launch an attack on us when their king is within our borders. You may rest easy, for I have sent out my soldiers to lead them to the palace. Since they are at the Northern borders, which is not much of a distance to the palace, I believe they shall be here soon. Please, you may sit whilst we await your men."

Ai watched as the younger king did as he was told. He then turned his amused gaze from her father to herself, where it rested in open admiration. She immediately looked away, unable to meet his eyes.

In a bid to draw his attention away from herself, she spoke the first thought that came to mind. "Father, whilst we await the men from the borders, may I ask what these rumours are that were spread about me before the ball?" The words were out before she could consider its consequences, but the look on her father's face was enough to know she had made an error.

"How did you come to know about the rumours, Ai?" Her father questioned in a futile effort to mask his pain. Ai blinked, unable to speak. She had asked it partly because she wanted a distraction from Johin's gaze but also because she wished him to know that she was not as undesirable as she had seemed in the ballroom. However, with further thoughts on the matter, she realised how bad it made her kingdom look.

"Yes, Your Majesty, I have been meaning to speak on the subject since after the ball but have not had the opportunity. Since the princess has brought it up, we may very well discuss it." A noble said before the princess could think of a way to change the subject.

"I agree," Another noble shouted. "When your majesty announced your desire to give our dear princess to be wed to an eligible bachelor in the Kingdom, it was of great joy to me. I was certain that my dear son would be the first to make known his suit."

Ai stared at the middle-aged man as he spoke, realising that the issue was about to be bigger than she expected, and it was out of her power to stop it. She felt her heartbeat increase with mortification as she wondered if she had disappointed her father.

"My son is well known for all the gifts and talents he possesses, and his beauty is only an added advantage to his eligibility. I am quite certain the princess would find him an agreeable young man," another nobleman stated.

"Even I cannot express the joy my son had when I told him about your announcement, as he began to prepare for the moment when he would finally make his suit known to the princess." A different nobleman spoke. "However, when that evil news began to spread, my Madame became concerned."

"Pray tell sir, what is this horrendous news you speak of?" Ai asked, and the entire room went silent. She could sense her father looking apprehensively in her direction, but she was too curious to cease her inquiry.

"The rumour, princess, was eh..." The man stuttered and went silent. Since she had first heard Duke Whall speak of the rumours, she had no time to consider the possible contents of the rumour. Although she had been determined to get to the bottom of the matter, she had chosen the worst time to speak of it and wished she had not brought it up in the presence of Johin.

"The rumours have variations, but it was implied that the Prophet told his majesty, that a deadly curse shall befall the family of whosoever shall wed you, your Highness." Lord Raine answered bluntly when no one else spoke.

Ai turned to her parents with a questioning look, but both averted their gazes. She turned to prophet Asher with a questioning gaze trying to ascertain if he had truly declared such a thing. The old man simply shook his head. She turned again to Lord Raine, who was scowling at her like she was a nuisance.

"And from whence has this rumour begun, sir?" Ai questioned, unsure if his disapproving look stemmed from the fact that she brought the matter up in the presence of foreigners, or guilt because he was the perpetrator. She watched him shift uncomfortably, as her tone held apparent accusation.

"Ahem..." The flustered noble coughed. For the first time since she had known him, he seemed unable to meet her eyes. "On the eve of the ball, anonymous letters containing the rumour were sent to the wives of several high-ranking nobles and some foreign guests."

Ai was perplexed at this revelation but did her best to maintain a calm disposition. "And to what end was this gossip spread, sir?" She was unable to fathom why anyone was so invested in destroying her honour that they would go as far as spreading such falsities.

"The answer to your question, your Highness, lies in the mind of the one who orchestrated such plans. My family was not privy to this information, for we did not receive the letter, and I never lend my ears to silly gossip. I have only heard of it from His Majesty."

"You will pardon me, sir, for you appeared to know all the details. Besides, I find it incredible that your family alone did not receive the letter."

The man opened his mouth in shock and turned to the king as though questioning why he was allowing her authority to champion the meeting. Ai, seeing the guilt-ridden look on her father's face, knew he would not be stopping her.

She turned from him to Lord Whall who was sitting with a solemn look. He caught her gaze and offered her a small smile, but she could see the sadness in his eyes. He was the only one who had felt the need to tell the king. If he had not done so, the matter might never have been brought up. She was thankful to him but knew she could not offer him her thanks, as that would mean her admitting to eavesdropping.

After some moments of silence in the room, Ai turned to the noble who had been speaking before Lord Raine. "You may continue."

"Yes, Your Highness. Despite the news, my son wished to come forward, but my wife made him vow that he would do no such thing. I should have commanded..."

The man's voice faded amidst her inward reflections. She tried to comprehend how dire the situation was and vaguely noticed when other nobles rose and gave similar opinions, speaking in favour of their children, or even themselves. Overwhelmed by all she was hearing, she desired to be away from the throne room and in her secret place, where she could hide from the feeling of being so unwanted.

At some point, the throne room became rowdy as almost every noble present had something to say and only a few noticed when the King lifted his hand to stop them.

"Silence!" The booming voice of Lord Raine echoed through the throne room, and Ai was startled at his outburst. "His Majesty, the King, shall address us."

The princess frowned at the man with ardent irritation. Most of the nobles present were his equals and she did not like how he addressed them like they were beneath him. Her dislike for him was as great as his for her, and she suspected that he had something to do with the rumours. Nonetheless, she could admit that he got their attention and directed them to the king.

"I have heard your arguments and can attest that most are valid and compelling. However, none of you thought it wise to make this rumour known to me before I made the grievous announcement at the ball. Also, despite the rumours, none of your gallant sons were brave enough to step out.

I can confirm to you that those rumours are baseless and untrue. On the contrary, I have been told by the prophet that whosoever shall win Princess Ai's heart shall be blessed and favoured. I have also vowed never to put my dear child through such an ordeal again. Hence, the choice of who to court and eventually wed shall solely be made by the princess. That is, with the blessing of the Prophet, of course." The King's irrefutable declaration stunned the entire room into a moment of silence.

At that moment, an Ore soldier announced that a dozen, out of the hundred men who had come seeking the Bamish king, had been allowed to enter the palace.

"Bring them to me." King James commanded, and the men were swiftly led into the room. After paying homage to their king, they turned to offer greetings to the king of Ore.

"Good sirs, I have been informed that you are nobles of Bamah. To what do we owe the pleasure of your visit?" King James questioned.

The group had puzzled expressions on their faces, as though questioning if he could not see the obvious. One of the men who looked like a dignified noble with his exquisite robes responded. "We have come to seek our king."

"Shall we say he was lost then?" King James asked comically.

"Well, er... I shall not say he was, sir..." The man started.

"You shall address our King as 'Your Majesty!'" Lord Raine thundered with evident anger.

Although a noble of Bamah, the man seemed intimidated by Lord Raine's' fury. His attitude and lack of manners, even towards guests, annoyed the princess greatly, and she did all to constrain herself from putting him in his place. Since she had earlier embarrassed her kingdom, she did not wish to do any further harm by giving the man an unrestrained piece of her mind.

"My sincere apologies, your Majesty, I meant no dishonour." The Bamish noble said sheepishly, looking warily from Lord Raine to the King of Ore. He went on to express that there were pressing issues in Bamah that king Johin needed to attend to, as he had been out of the kingdom for almost two weeks.

"What shall you say to this, young king?" King James questioned. "It appears you have some urgent business and shall be unable to continue courtship with my daughter."

Again, the noble stepped forward and spoke. "Forgive my imprudence, your Majesty. The royal advisors of Bamah have requested, if your majesty would permit it, that the princess return with us to Bamah. We are aware of our king's declaration to the princess and shall consider her presence a diplomatic visit, where they may continue their courtship, as the King goes about his duties."

She turned to her father and noticed his clenched jaw as he frowned at the Bamish noble. If looks could kill, the man would have ceased to exist in that moment.

THIRTEEN

Ai felt her heart race in excitement at the mere thought of leaving Ore borders. Her father had never permitted her to go beyond the City of Belleich, where the palace was situated.

"That is a splendid plan!" King Johin proclaimed. "It shall be an opportunity for the princess to explore my kingdom, as I have hers. It would signify peace between our kingdoms. "

Ai saw that the eagerness in Johin's eyes was not reflected in her father's. Instead, his frown deepened, and she was certain a refusal was imminent. However, when he opened his mouth to speak, he paused and turned to her with an inscrutable expression.

"You have my word that she would be cared for and protected as though it were you, your Majesty." Johin pursued.

King James turned to him and spoke so softly that Ai almost missed his words. "The decision on this matter shall be made by the princess."

Ai gasped at his words. It was surreal that he was giving her the choice. She was uncertain if his motive was to prove a point to the Bamish people, or to make up for his actions during the ball, but she could without doubt comprehend that the look in his eyes was a silent plea for her to reject the offer.

She turned to her mother hoping she would share her excitement but was instead met with a gaze that held both fear and anger. Ai could easily recognise that the queen was furious at the ludicrous declaration and was frightened about the inevitable outcome. She watched as her mother shook her head slightly, silently pleading with her to refuse, but she turned from her and back to her father.

"Thank you, Father, for your kind consideration. It shall be my utmost pleasure to serve Ore with a diplomatic visit to Bamah," she said calmly, afraid she would burst with excitement if she said anymore.

"I feared you would say that." King James said unenthusiastically, doing little to hide his disappointment. "There are some conditions to this, nonetheless."

Ai gave him a knowing look. "And what are these conditions, father?"

"I shall choose at least a hundred Ore soldiers and a dozen trained servants to go with you. Your grandmother also shall go with you as chaperone. You must return before the anniversary of my coronation. Hence, you have less than a month, including your travel time." King James declared.

Ai considered his words thoughtfully. The conditions were not as harsh as she expected. She loved her grandmother dearly and would have chosen her as a chaperone if her father had not. She however could not like the idea of soldiers and servants swarming her, every step of the way.

"Father, if I have Michael follow and watch over me as he did at the festival, would you cut down the number of people assigned to me?" she asked and her father took a moment to consider it, his fingers sweeping through his greying beards.

"I shall allow it and give you fifty soldiers instead." Ai heard her mother gasp and willed herself not to look at her.

"Please Father, a dozen skilled soldiers and one hand maiden would suffice. It is a diplomatic trip and not a war after all. I am certain that King Johin's men would ensure my safety.

"Two dozen men Ai, and that is my final word!"

"Then, I shall say no more, but offer my gratitude," she responded smiling. She had purposefully asked for the low numbers so her father could give her a reasonable number.

"You may leave at dawn tomorrow." King James said solemnly and dismissed the meeting. The princess arose and excused herself from the gathering, stating that she needed to make haste to begin preparations for her travels.

All hopes of avoiding her mother till she was mentally prepared were dashed when the queen offered to go with her to help with the preparations. The queen said nothing else till they were safely in her bedchamber.

"You wicked child, have you no care at all for my heart?" She asked, looking as though she would weep.

"Mother! Surely you did not expect that I would refuse such an unprecedented opportunity. You know that father would never again in my lifetime put such an offer forward. It was in fact, only because he was so ridden with guilt, that this good fortune came about. I for one thought you would be excited for me."

"Excited?" Her mother questioned, exasperatedly. "How could I be, knowing my only child is going on such a shocking adventure with only two dozen men? I assure you that I shall be unable to close my eyes a wink each day you are gone."

"Mother, I am quite convinced that king John would ensure I do not come to any harm."

"Well, that is no help, since I do not know the man nor have the least bit of faith in his ability to keep you safe. My only consolation is that Michael shall be at your side. I dearly wish to change your mind and make you stay." She said with a hopeful look. Ai shook her head and embraced her saddened parent.

"You may rest easy Mother, for I know Michael shall vexatiously follow me everywhere as he did at the love festival, and as you know, I shall remain under the refuge of the Almighty."

These words seemed to calm her parent into acquiescence, as no further efforts were made to dissuade her from her decision. Instead, her mother helped choose the best dresses and accessories suitable for a diplomatic visit.

By noon the following day, the princess was out of Ore's borders. She sat in a carriage with her grandmother and her younger handmaiden. Since her father had not insisted on her taking servants, she only took the twenty-five Ore soldiers, including her knight who rode beside their carriage.

She had been able to convince her grandmother that Surina was sufficient to serve the two of them along the way, and the Bamish servants will serve them in Bamah. In truth, she had opted to take only one handmaiden with her, as she had no other trusted servants she wished to accompany her. Johin had assured her that morning, that there would be more than enough at her service in Bamah.

Ai squealed in excitement as she watched the trees go by the windows of the carriage. "Oh grandmother, is it not all so beautiful?" She asked, awestruck.

"It is just a forest child," Eva responded with a smile.

"Well, I have never seen any forests beyond Ore, and none so wild," Ai responded and stared out of the carriage window again.

She recalled the tearful look on her mother's face that morning as she prepared to leave and swallowed the guilt she felt for ignoring her mother's wishes. She was going to a kingdom that offered an acceptance she had longed for since she was a child. Her first-ever friends were from that kingdom. She was also being offered the promise of a marriage she had never dared to dream of. Her mother could never understand the pains of being consistently disapproved.

"I hear the Kingdom of Bamah is so beautiful that people from all over the world would travel weeks and months, just to behold its beauty. However, after the Yachad festival, it closed its borders to outsiders. Oh, what a great honour to be able to see it." Surina said with a dreamy look on her face. Ai had opted to take her instead of Martha since she did not want the woman to embark on such a journey, whilst she was with child.

"It is indeed as you say." her grandmother's voice broke through her thoughts, as she responded to Surina.

"Have you ever been there, grandmother?" Ai questioned in surprise.

"In the past... " Eva started but burst into a fit of coughing.

"Grandmother!" Ai shrieked, frightened by this. Her grandmother began to frantically search her satchel. "Whatever is the matter, grandmother?" Ai questioned in an alarming tone. "Stop the carriage!" she yelled, hitting it with urgency. The carriage did stop, and Ai could see Michael bring his horse to stop beside it.

Surina sat beside Eva, patting her back. "I seem to have forgotten my medicine, child." the ageing woman said when her coughing fit was over. She was red with distress and Ai put the back of her hands against her grandmother's temples.

"You are burning with fever, grandmother. Why have you not told me that you are ill?" The princess questioned in a shaken voice.

"I did not wish to ruin your first chance to go outside Ore, especially since you were so enthused by the idea. I was quite certain that your father would never let you leave, if I did not go with you." She coughed again and began wheezing.

"We must return to Ore at once," Ai said, ignoring the feeling of disappointment she felt.

"Nonsense, child. I... I shall survive this... no need to end your trip... for such a trivial issue." Eva said, amidst her wheezing.

"I shall take no wager with your life, for you are far more valuable than some adventure away from Ore."

A knock on the carriage window caused Ai to look from her grandmother to see the Bamish King's expression of concern. He opened the carriage door, and with a sweeping gaze inside, he spoke.

"Is all well, dear Ai?"

"Please accept my sincere apologies, King John, but I must return to the palace at once. My grandmother is quite ill and has forgotten to take her medication with her."

"We have the best physicians at Bamah, so you can be assured that she would be seen to, on our arrival."

Ai shot him an incredulous look. "Nothing shall prevail on me to undertake such a foolish risk with my grandmother's life."

"Then I must return to Ore alone," Eva intervened. Her wheezing had ended, but her voice was hoarse, and she looked as though she would pass out at any time.

"I shall not allow it, grandmother!" Ai cried, horrified by the notion. "Who shall care for you along the way?"

"I shall go with Surina. You shall have the maids in Bamah who would care for your needs." Eva responded.

"Oh grandmother, I shall be sick with worry if I do not return with you."

"Dear child, I do not see why you should, for I do not intend to die for many years. I do not think your parents would be so benevolent to grant you such a second opportunity as this if you do return to Ore. It shall not be on my account that you miss this adventure."

Ai knew there was a lot of truth in her grandmother's words and wavered on her resolve to return to Ore with the older woman. Whilst her father had not voiced it, she could tell that he wanted nothing more but for her to remain in Ore. Her mother had not hidden her sentiments against the trip.

"I give you my word child, as soon as I arrive at my house outside the palace, I shall send a trusted messenger to put your mind at ease. If you do not receive any word from me within a week, you may contrive to return to Ore at an earlier date than agreed."

"But father would be incensed that I have no chaperone,"

"You have your knight, and I am aware he has the absolute trust of the king. I shall delay in telling him of my presence lest he orders your immediate return. That should buy you some time to enjoy the goodness of Bamah, sweet child." The older woman said, putting her palm on the cheek of the princess in a loving manner.

"Your grandmother may return in my carriage. I shall ride with one of my noble men." Johin offered, he had a look of hope in his eyes, as though silently convincing her not to leave.

Whilst it felt like an amazing opportunity to continue her adventure, she could not shake off the burden on her conscience. It felt like she would be disappointing her parents and even betraying her grandmother if she continued to Bamah. In that moment, she desired nothing, but the wise counsel of her knight.

FOURTEEN

Ai glanced gloomily outside the carriage window, unable to fully appreciate the sights before her. Her heart was heavy, and she was only comforted by the knowledge that whatever choice she made, she would have been saddened by it. All the beauty she beheld within the Bamish borders was not enough to lift her spirits.

She had ordered a dozen of the Ore soldiers to return with her grandmother and obtained a promise that none of the soldiers will be sent back to her. She requested a person from the palace who did not embark on the trip to reassure her that the woman had truly arrived safely.

At the time, she had given half of her soldiers to alleviate the guilt of not returning with her grandmother. However, on reflection after separating from the elderly woman, she realised that it would be very upsetting to her father, especially since he had wanted her to go with a hundred men at first.

"Do you think I did wrong, Michael?" She had asked her knight, when they stopped to rest.

"There is a thin line between right and wrong, Your Highness. One can only determine what is right or wrong, based on what they truly believe." Ai had waited in vain for him to explain further, but he did not, and that left her even more disturbed as she pondered on his words.

They arrived at the Bamish palace after three days of travel. She almost forgot all her worries at the sight of the grand structure. The array of flowers, exquisite architecture and the magnificent sculptures that beautified the great building, were better than all she had envisioned.

"I hope our shabby kingdom is to your liking, my dear Ai." She heard Johin say from behind her and turned to him, she was spared from offering any response as a female voice called out from behind her.

"Brother! You have returned." Ai abruptly turned again to see a strikingly beautiful woman come up towards them. She had a slender but shapely figure that was complimented by her elegant dress. Her fair face bore a most welcoming expression, and her dark hair and blue eyes were undeniable features of her identity. She stopped in her strides as soon as her gaze fell upon Ai and a look of surprise graced her face.

"Ai?" She questioned softly.

"Hana?" Ai questioned and the woman stepped forward and pulled her into a long embrace.

"Isa." She said as she broke the embrace. "That is my real name. Isa. I never had the opportunity to tell it to you."

"Isa." Ai repeated smiling.

"Oh, my dear friend, you have blossomed into the most beautiful flower," Isa said, pulling back to observe her in admiration.

"I must say the same of you Hana... Isa." Ai did not doubt that it would take some time to get familiar with the name.

"Oh, how I missed you and longed for the day we could meet again and do all we did together," Isa said.

"Alas, dear friend, I am afraid we might be too old to play hide and seek now." Ai jested and received a most melodious laughter that warmed her heart. She could hardly contain her joy, as she perceived that her friend's personality had not changed much, since they last were together.

"I understand, dear Isa, that you have not seen our beloved friend in so many years and there is much to speak about, but we have journeyed many hours, and I am certain that the princess is exhausted. Would you lead her to the best chambers and ensure that she is tended to by our best servants?" Johin requested, interrupting their little moment.

"Of course, brother. I must welcome you as well. I am glad you are safely home, for your wretched advisors have not let me have a moment of peace. Come now, Ai, I shall make certain that you have the best experience in our..." Isa stopped speaking, and stared dazed, beyond Ai.

Ai turned around to see the reason Isa had ceased speaking and noticed that Michael had taking his place, standing close behind her. "Michael, stand down, you cruel being. Do you not see that you are frightening the princess?" She said laughing, as she realised that her giant-looking knight who stood at least six feet and five inches tall was not a happy sight to people who did not know of him.

"You would recall the promise you made to the king, princess. It is on his authority that I follow you so closely." the man responded.

"It is of no consequence, Ai, for I am not at all frightened..." Isa began saying but was interrupted by the incensed voice of her brother.

"Sir, you would do well to recognise that you are now within Bamah territory, where I am king, and I say you do as your princess says." He ordered, and Ai observed the unmistakable annoyance in his expression.

As expected, Michael, ignored his words and did not spare him a glance. This did not surprise the Ore princess, since it will be out of character for him to take orders from anyone, but the royalty of Ore. He had time and again, snubbed the Ore nobles and had gone as far as rebuffing their orders or scaring them away with his intimidating stares.

Ai sighed in defeat. "Please accept my sincere apologies, but I did give my word to my father to have my knight always by me, and I have defied him enough on our journey here."

"Shall we dine together at dusk tomorrow, Ai?" the king asked, looking as though he was struggling to maintain his calm disposition. The princess did not know what she could say to alleviate his annoyance, so she simply nodded. She was unwilling to reprove her knight since he had done nothing that could be deemed as wrong. "Well then, I shall entrust you into the hands of my sister, and leave you to rest till dinner tomorrow, whilst I attend to my long-neglected duties." He offered her a small smile before he went with some of his men into the palace.

The Bamish princess ordered some servants to tend to the Ore soldiers and led Ai to a room with two large doors. "This shall be your chambers for as long as you're with us," she said, as two servants opened them to reveal the room.

It was almost as large as a ballroom. It had beautiful curtains, expensive furnishings, and engravings around the walls. There was a large bed in the middle with gold frames and exquisite-looking beddings. There was also a pool to the side of the room, with curtains around it.

She found the room rather eerie, and could not bring herself to like it, as she was certain servants would always be in and out to maintain its ambience. She was tempted to request a smaller room, but did not wish to offend her friend.

"Thank you, Isa. This is indeed a magnificent room. If it is not too much to ask, I would like a bath to be prepared, for I am quite weary from the journey and would love nothing better than a warm bath and a quiet rest."

Isa ensured that her servants did as was requested before leaving with a promise to see the princess by noon the next day.

"I shall remain outside your chambers, Princess," Michael said after Isa had left.

"Surely you must be tired, Michael, riding a horse for so many hours. You must rest."

"I cannot rest till I am certain you are safe, and within these borders, I do not trust that you are." He responded simply.

"In that case, you should take turns with other soldiers. How can you protect me when you are worn out in strength?" She asked and watched her knight lean back as if considering what she said. He stared intently at her, and she resisted the urge to turn away. Whilst she had never been intimidated by him, his gaze usually made her feel like he could see her innermost thoughts. "Do as you wish Michael." She said and allowed the maids close the doors and tend to her.

When she was finally alone, the princess had enough time to reflect on her situation. Her mind drifted to her grandmother, and she said a silent prayer, hoping the sickly woman returned safely to Ore and was well. She did not know when she fell asleep, but the next time she opened her eyes, it was Isa, who was hovering over her and calling her name.

FIFTEEN

The princess used her hand to block out the light streaming through the windows, as Isa walked over and opened the curtains.

"Forgive me, Ai. I understand that you were weary from your journey, but I feared you were dead since you were sleeping so soundly, despite all that was going on around you." Isa explained with a smile, as Ai sat up on the bed. Indeed, there were several servants in and out of the room.

"What hour of the day is it?"

"It's an hour past noon," Isa replied.

Ai shot up from the bed. She had never slept so late in her life, and for so many hours. The smell of incense filled the room. It was a sweet smell, so calming that Ai almost gave in to the temptation of going back to sleep. Isa encouraged her to enjoy every waking hour in Bamah, then ordered the servants to serve her.

Within an hour Ai was ready for the day. Although she could appreciate that the maidservants in Bamah were very efficient, they did not know what to do with her hair. After several tries, the princess insisted on styling it herself, and did so in the simplest way she had learned, with many hair accessories that made it glamorous enough to befit her title. Michael was at her door and bowed as soon as she stepped out.

"Did you get a good rest, Michael?" She asked with a smile.

"Yes princess, I had enough rest to remain by your side for the rest of your stay on this foreign soil, just as you promised the King." Ai nodded hastily, reminded of her father and his probable reaction to her grandmother's return. "The Bamish princess has requested that you have a meal with her in her garden."

In a matter of minutes, Ai was seated with Isa in a beautiful and well-kept flower garden, with a table of food before them.

"I thank you, Michael, for delivering my request." The Bamish royal said in a cheery tone to the knight who stood at the entrance of the garden.

"You seem more at ease with my knight, dear Isa. You appeared quite frightened of him yesterday." Ai said and watched in confusion as her friend turned red.

"Oh... Ahem!" The Bamish princess stuttered but cleared her throat and spoke again in a whisper. "It was less of fright and more of awe, Ai. You must know that your knight is a shockingly beautiful man."

Ai choked on the goblet of fresh orange juice. "Of what do you speak, Isa?" she questioned dabbing her lips with a napkin.

"Surely you know that your knight possesses the most beautiful features. Not only that, but he is also strongly built and gallant. I must own that he is quite reserved, which does not suit me at all, for I should have thrown caution and title to the wind for him." Ai gazed in bewilderment as her friend spoke so freely and inadvertently turned to gaze at the man in question, hoping to the heavens that he could not hear their conversation. "He is the most gorgeous man I have ever seen in my life!" Isa squealed.

Ai turned to Isa, giving her a blank look. She had heard from Surina time and again that Michael was the most handsome in the palace but had never given much thought to it. She was spared from uttering any response when a Bamish servant walked up to Isa and whispered in her ears.

"Forgive me, Ai, I must attend to some matters in the palace," Isa said, offered her apologies, and left with the servant.

Although Isa gave her the liberty to use the palace servants and guards at will, Ai opted to walk around the palace with Michael. She found that she was unable to resist the urge to stare at him, as Isa's comment rang repeatedly in her head. She tried in vain to observe him discreetly but was always caught by his ever-so-ready gaze.

"Are you well, princess?" He asked after he caught her eyes the third time. The princess nodded but decided to stop and openly stare at him since she had failed in her attempt to be discreet.

Michael frowned, "Have you something to say to me? Are you displeased by my overbearing presence? Or is it the manner I regarded the king–"

"No Michael, it is none of that. I should hope to call you to book on those matters in the future, but at this moment, I am simply trying to observe you." She said candidly.

"To what end?"

"I shall rather drown myself in a river than disclose my reasons to you, good sir." his brows shot up briefly, but the short-lived surprise was replaced by a blank look, as he folded his arms.

"If you intend to sell me. I can assure you that you are wasting your time, for–"

"Oh, hush Michael. I do not know from whence you conjure such ridiculous notions, but I do wonder if your mind suffers periodic abnormalities."

"Alas, dear princess, we share similar views of each other."

"Michael, you goose! How dare you say such a thing to your princess." She said laughing.

"Why, do you desire to sell me now? Do not worry, I shall oblige you as soon as you are safely returned home." Ai suddenly stopped laughing and a serious look replaced her mirth.

"Michael! I shall never trade you for any cost, and you shall do well to not provoke me by jesting about such an odious thing."

She turned from him angrily with the hope of returning to her chambers but was obliged to ask him for directions. It was therefore with evident amusement, much to her chagrin, that he led her.

By the time Isa came to her that evening, Ai was well-rested and prepared for dinner. She was thankful to the servants who dressed her. Not one seemed to disapprove of her, nor notice her complexion. She walked into the dining room hand in hand with her friend and was amazed at the delicacies on the table. Johin was already at the table, and he rose as the ladies walked in, followed closely by Michael.

"Surely, you do not truly intend to follow the princess everywhere," Johin said to Michael, with an edge in his voice.

"It is of no consequence, brother. He is simply ensuring Ai's safety," Isa said as she took her place at the table.

"The princess is safe within our borders!" He said curtly then turned to Ai and spoke in a softer tone. "I do hope you have been well looked after, Ai."

"Yes, very much so. Your servants are very efficient." She responded, wishing eagerly to get past the tension in the room. Since Michael was only following her father's orders based on her request, she could not fault him for it, regardless of how much it provoked Johin.

"May we eat? I am quite famished." Isa said.

"Yes, we may," Johin responded, and the servants began serving.

"Shan't we say a blessing over the food?" She asked, just before anyone had an opportunity to eat. Johin gave her a questioning look, then smirked.

"You may bless the food, Ai," he said simply. Ai looked at him sceptically but closed her eyes and prayed over the food.

It was a quiet dinner and Ai noticed Johin's watchful gaze on her. When she caught his eyes, he did not look away. She recalled her father's words about how royalty turns away from no one and decided to take on the challenge by holding his gaze.

"Why do you not sit and dine, Michael? Surely you must be famished," Isa said, breaking the silence. Johin tore his gaze from Ai's and gave his sister an incredulous look like she had taken leave of her senses.

"I forbid it!" He yelled angrily.

"I shall dine with my men," Michael responded simply, and Ai was thankful Isa did not insist, since the mutual dislike between the men was quite evident. The dinner ended with only a small amount of the food getting eaten.

"Shall we take a private walk in the garden, Ai?" Johin requested.

"In that case, I shall bid you goodnight and see you tomorrow my dear friend," Isa said, rising. She offered Ai a smile and left the room.

Johin arose and offered Ai his hand which she took and let him lead her. As they walked to the passage, Michael followed behind them, much to the king's chagrin. Ai could see him tense up in annoyance and after a few steps, he turned to him and spoke.

"For the Lord's sake, would you not give us a private moment?" He yelled.

For the first time that evening, Michael regarded the king, but even Ai could observe that it was in a most condescending manner. He stared down at the slightly shorter man with a most intimidating look.

"No." He responded simply.

SIXTEEN

Ai fidgeted with the sides of her skirts, distressed to be in the middle of the two tall men, who looked ready to battle. She knew she needed to intervene before it was too late.

"Please Michael, do give us a little private moment. I am convinced Johin would not let me fall to harm." Michael gave her a questioning look. "I command it!" She added firmly before he could dispute.

Michael stared into her eyes for a moment, then bowed and walked away. Ai felt a pang of guilt at this. She knew she was going against what she agreed with her father, but she could tell that Johin was losing his patience with Michael's blatant disregard for his status. She did not know what the consequences of consistently dishonouring a King were in Bamah, and she did not wish to find out.

Ai allowed Johin to lead her into the garden, which was well-lit with several unique lamps that shone brightly in the dark. They were beautiful, but after the events that occurred a few moments before, she could not be fascinated by them. The Bamish king had remained silent as they walked, leaving her to dwell guiltily on her errors. In Ore, she would never have been allowed to walk alone at night with Johin, even if her grandmother had been with her as a chaperone.

Johin suddenly stopped walking, and Ai was compelled to do the same.

"My dearest Ai, may I say how pleased I am to be rid of that loathsome fellow. He is like a buzzing insect that never leaves till completely crushed."

Ai's brows dipped as she pondered his harsh words towards Michael. She considered expressing that the said man was the knight to whom she owed her life but was taken aback by his next words.

"I am undoubtedly in love with you, Ai." He declared, taking her hand and holding it to his chest. Ai blinked in surprise and reflexively tried to pull away, but his strong grip prevented it. "You may not understand it yet, but I am quite convinced you feel the same way towards me. I could see it in your eyes when our gazes locked at dinner."

The princess was unsure of how the supposed staring contest had been misconstrued as affection. She did not know what the love between a man and a woman felt like, so she had never thought to check her feelings towards him.

He was undeniably a beautiful man, and even Surina had told her that the fame of his looks, and power, was known all over the world. She felt a burst of pride at the idea of being loved by such a man but did not know if what she felt was the same as the love she had read in books or seen in her parents.

"Ai?" Johin called softly, a questioning look on his face. Ai blinked as she realised that she had been absently staring into his eyes whilst her mind took a journey.

"Ahem... " She stuttered. "Forgive me, Johin, for I am unable to make such a bold declaration as you have. I am inexperienced and uncertain of how love should feel."

"Then, allow me to teach you the true meaning of love," he said, lifting her hand to his lips and kissing it. Ai was so dazed by his actions that she barely registered when his other hand went around her waist and pulled her closer to himself. He dropped her hand and lifted her chin so that they were gazing into each other's eyes. It was not until she felt his breath on her face that she realised that their lips were inches apart. She abruptly pulled away, feeling faint with embarrassment as she realised that he had almost kissed her.

"I... I must retire now, as I am quite weary from walking around your palace." She turned from him and briskly walked out of the garden before he could stop her. She was most pleased to see six Ore's soldiers awaiting her in the passage and they bowed at the sight of her.

"We have been ordered to escort you to your chambers, your Highness," One of them explained and Ai nodded. She did not know why Michael felt the need to send six soldiers as his replacement, but she was grateful to be away from Johin.

Alone in her assigned chambers, Ai tried to reflect on the events of the evening, but it soon became overshadowed by the thoughts of her grandmother. She recalled in melancholy that she had not received the promised messenger and reflected in deep anxiety the possibility that she had not returned safely. She was certain their company would have arrived at Ore, long before she got to Bamah.

She shuddered at the image of her parents when they discovered she had persisted in travelling to Bamah with no chaperone and half the number of soldiers agreed. She found solace in her decision to return to Ore, if she received no message in a week.

The next morning, Ai again had difficulty waking up early and had to be gently roused by a Bamish maidservant an hour before noon. She attributed it to her restlessness the previous night. The calming scent in the room made the princess want to lay in bed with no worries but she resisted it and allowed the servants to ready her for the day.

Michael was at the door when she stepped out and she suddenly felt the weight of her words and actions the previous evening. She wished she could escape the awkwardness and return to their usual friendly banter.

"Are you well, princess?" He questioned with an air of indifference. Ai nodded, slowly sparing him a glance.

"Did you get enough rest?" she asked, resisting the urge to cower under his intense gaze.

"I am strong enough to never leave your side again." He said bluntly. Ai frowned and was about to protest, but recalling all that happened the previous evening, she nodded repentantly.

"Michael..." She began, eager to offer apologies for how curt she had been with him.

"Shall I lead you to where the Bamish princess awaits?"

Ai looked up at him and saw a small smile on his face as though he was aware that she was contrite about the previous night. Isa's voice suddenly rang in her head.

Surely you have noticed what a beautiful man Michael is...

She immediately turned away from him, as she came to the realisation that he indeed looked quite dashing whenever he smiled.

"Well, what is it now?" the knight asked, with evident amusement.

"I am quite ashamed of how shabbily I treated you yesterday." She replied hastily, fearing he would know what she was thinking with his extraordinary perceptiveness.

"Well, you should be," he responded, and she abruptly turned back to him in surprise, and saw him smirking.

"You are an abominable person, Michael. Surely you know to respond politely to such a humble apology."

"Was that an apology? Forgive me, I thought you were expressing the shame you felt for treating me shabbily." His grin was infectious, causing her to smile against her wish.

"Of all the provoking things to say– Well, I shall not dwell on the matter, but I do beg your pardon, dear Michael. I am very aware that in sending you away, I have broken my word to my father. But I knew not what to do, with you incensing the king in such an odious way, I did not wish to fan the flames any further."

"Well, ma'am, perhaps you should not try to fight my battles."

"Michael, you must know he is a king, and you are within his territory. Whilst I am quite confident in your physical prowess, I do not wish to test it against a thousand men. And please, do not call me by that odious title! Why, you only say it when you mean to provoke me."

"I mean no such thing, Your Highness, but if it puts your mind at ease, I shall contrive to be more civil with the Bamish king. He must also respect that I am doing my duty as your knight." Ai sighed knowing that neither man would be willing to concede to the other. She simply asked to be led to Isa and put the matter out of her mind.

The two princesses sat in a small room with a light luncheon and shared their experiences growing up in their different kingdoms. The Ore royal was happy to speak of Martha, Nathan, Michael and Surina whom she regarded as her friends and confidants. She empathised better with Isa who had quite the opposite of her experiences, but just as bad. Whilst the Bamish princess was highly revered by her people, she had been proportionately neglected by her parents, as though her existence was a nuisance.

She decided to change the conversation to the less depressing subject, of the mischievous and amusing things she did with Nathan, growing up. Isa expressed her awe at the liberties she was given and how she was doted upon.

"I wish I had your parents, for I hated mine." Ai was spared the obligation to respond to the shocking revelation, as a palace maid walked into the room and curtsied. She then proceeded to whisper something to Isa.

"It appears that a messenger has arrived from Ore," Isa said as the maid backed away. Ai's hands involuntarily went up to her heart as it began to pound heavily. She hoped to the heavens that it was not a messenger of doom.

"Please Isa, if it is not too much to ask, desire him to come hither."

Isa nodded and turned to the maid. "Send him here directly,"

Ai struggled to breathe as various thoughts crossed her mind. She rose and began to pace about the room. *Could it be evil tidings about her grandmother, or from her father?* Each minute felt like an eternity as she waited. She abandoned any idea of continuing with the meal before her, as her appetite was diminished by anxiety. She vaguely heard Isa's futile attempt at soothing her with calming words.

She noticed Michael raising a questioning brow at her but was too anxious to consider him. After what felt like ages to the princess, two Bamish soldiers entered the room with a man in the middle of them. Ai turned from her pacing to see a familiar face.

"Nathan!" She squealed. It took all her will to restrain herself from running to embrace him.

SEVENTEEN

Nathan waved to her with a smile as he walked into the room. As though he recalled where he was, he cleared his throat and bowed.

"Your Highness," He greeted.

"How is my grandmother, Nathan?" She asked desperately, wishing to settle her immediate concern.

"She told me to assure you that she is well, so you may be at ease,"

Ai let out a sigh of relief, gladdened that all her fears had come to nought. Then a thought crossed her mind, that made her frown.

"And my father?"

Nathan blinked and looked around at the servants and soldiers present with meaning in his action, which the princess was quick to understand.

"Isa, if you please, I would like a private moment." She asked, but after a moment of no response, she looked in time to see her friend observing Nathan with evident awe. It wasn't till she called the second time that her friend turned away.

"Ah, yes," She responded, her cheeks turning a bright shade of red, as she dismissed the servants. "Do you also wish that I leave?"

"No, Isa. You may stay if you desire, for I have already told you the whole." She responded with a smile.

When the last of the servants had left the room Ai proceeded to throw herself into Nathan's arms. "Dearest Nathan, I did not, for the life of me, think I could ever miss your provoking presence." She said and released him.

"I should not know if you are offering compliments or throwing out insults, Ai. Never mind that, where is Michael? I do not believe he has left you alone, despite your father–" He was interrupted by a heavy slap at the back of his head, and he groaned in pain. Ai laughed at this as he turned around, holding his assaulted head. "Surely sir, you must know that there are less painful methods to make your presence known?"

"Forgive me puppy, but this way appears most effective." The knight responded and stretched out his hands. "I am glad you are well, Nathan."

"Of course you are! Only so you may kill me with your very hand." The man muttered in response but shook his hand, nonetheless.

"Perhaps if you had better perception, you would have easily dodged the blow."

Nathan smiled. "Perhaps if you choose to teach me as I have requested a thousand times, I will not be so oblivious."

"Such skills are not taught. They are innate and can be groomed by any who is willing," Michael responded coolly.

"I am glad to see that the foreign winds have not changed you, for you remain as dull as ever!" Nathan said dryly and got another strike on his head. "You are truly going to kill me if you keep doing that! Ai, put this lion on a leash, will you!" He yelled and Ai laughed out loud.

"Michael, you shall indeed be sorry if you truly kill poor Nathan. But Nathan, the last time I scolded Michael, for such a brutish act, you did all to appear tough." She responded in amusement.

"Well, that was before I saw sense and truth in your words. Upon my word, I should swoon if I get hit again." Ai was still laughing when she recalled the presence of her friend and turned to her.

"Forgive me, Isa, we must appear to be quite shocking, but I lay the blame at Nathan's door. I do not know how he contrives to make us appear so silly." She said, ignoring the look she was getting from Nathan.

"Not at all, dear Ai, I am more so fascinated." She responded kindly, then leaned in and whispered, "Although you told me of it, I have never seen subjects speak so freely in the presence of a royal. It is even more shocking to see your stoic knight jesting."

"Well, they are my friends and have been for so long. And, oh, how rude of me, I must introduce you to this provoking man."

"Is this the Nathan you spoke of in your tale? The one who finds joy in teasing you, but always fails." Isa asked aloud.

"Now Ai, that is no kind way to describe me in my absence, is it?" Nathan spoke instead. "I am indeed Nathan of the Ore kingdom, pleased to make your acquaintance, ma'am." He said, taking her hand and brushing his lips over the back of it.

"Nathan, this is Isa, princess of Bamah," Ai answered when she realised her friend had suddenly become unable to speak, and had turned a darker shade of red. She wondered not only at Isa's reaction but at Nathan's actions. She had never thought him to be chivalrous.

"What about my father Nathan?" Ai asked when she noticed that he was gazing at the Bamish princess and holding on to her hand for far too long. She did not wish to discomfit her royal friend by this side of Nathan that even she, was a stranger to.

"Yes, Ai," Nathan said absently, slowly turning to her and reluctantly releasing the princess. He gave her a dry look as though she had interrupted a most interesting vision. "Your grandmother sent me here in secrecy. She desires to give you some time before the king finds out and sends a legion of Ore soldiers to bring you safely home." Ai smiled approvingly at this, knowing her father was well capable of doing so, but immediately reconsidered.

Although she was glad that she was given such a rare opportunity to leave Ore, an oppressive feeling of guilt encompassed her. She had no wish to deceive her father. He was sometimes overbearing in his dotage but had always been the best parent anyone could pray for. He taught her most of what she knew and gave all the fatherly love that was almost comparable to the good Father in the Holy book. He most assuredly did not deserve her deception. And her poor mother...

"I must send a letter to my grandmother at once. My father must be told of my current circumstance." Ai stated urgently. She shuddered, as she imagined her mother's woeful reaction when she discovered her child was without a chaperone and with just over a dozen soldiers in a foreign land.

On request, Isa called for a servant to make all Ai needed available to her. After she had written and sealed the letter, she handed it over to Michael. "Please Michael, desire one of your soldiers to deliver my message to my grandmother speedily." Michael nodded and with a brief word to Nathan that he was under no circumstance to leave her side, he went off to carry out the order.

When he returned, Ai requested Isa to kindly see that Nathan was cared for, insisting he remain with her in Bamah. Isa obliged and got a servant to see to the man's lodging in the comforts of the palace. After the matter was settled, Ai obtained a promise from Nathan that he would take a long rest. She then left him to take a walk with Isa in the palace gardens.

"Pardon my inquisitiveness, Ai, I daresay you might find it rude that I ask, but I shall die of curiosity if I do not," Isa spoke in a low tone as they walked, doing her best to ensure she was not heard by the knight behind them. "Am I precise in my assumption that you and Nathan are secret lovers?" Ai shrieked and burst into a fit of laughter. Whilst she was slowly becoming accustomed to Isa's straight-talking, she could not help but be amused by it.

"Why on earth would you assume such a thing, Isa?"

"Well, for one, you both seemed rather comfortable in each other's company. Also, I shall let you know that I have read several books, and it appears that secret love between a royal and a subject is not unusual…"

"We are most certainly not lovers." Ai interrupted firmly, unwilling to hear any more. Whilst the idea of a relationship with the beautiful Nathan was not necessarily repugnant, she just could not stomach the thought. "The limit of our relationship is nothing beyond sibling affection"

There was a brief expression of relief on the face of the Bamish princess, which Ai did not miss.

"Is there perhaps a special reason you wished to know of my relationship with Nathan?" She asked smirking. Isa shook her head vehemently but was betrayed by her reddening cheeks. "Could it be, dear Isa, that you have taken a liking to Nathan?" she questioned, and Isa gasped and shook her head again. "Could this be what the books refer to as, er, love at first sight?"

"Oh Ai, why do you tease me so?" Isa replied, both hands covering her flustered face. Ai began to giggle in amusement. "I do not know how you remain so composed and surrounded by such beautiful men." The flustered woman whispered. Ai's brows furrowed as she considered this.

"Perhaps it is because I have known them for so long. Nathan is such a provoking tease, that I sometimes am tempted to smack him in the head as Michael does. And Michael..." Ai paused to think, "I guess he is just Michael– as provoking, as he is gallant."

"I can understand it. Your knight is quite reserved in his ways and has such a cool intimidating air. I was quite amazed to see him speak more than a few words today. Nathan on the other hand has a wonderful charisma that makes him quite endearing. Tell me, Ai, do you know if he is betrothed to anyone?" Isa asked, suddenly confident.

Ai put her finger on her chin in deep thought. She had never thought to ask Nathan or Michael if they had any romantic attachments. "I am afraid I do not know the answer to that question. I possess no knowledge of him being betrothed to anyone, and he seemed quite taken with you. I have never seen him look at anyone the way he did you."

"Do you think, Ai?" Isa asked in uncontained excitement. "He reminds me very much of my instructor in the Nichi Kingdom. At the time, though a child, I fancied myself in love with him and always dreamt of running away to wed him." She laughed at this reflection and added, "It was he who called us by the names we told you of."

Ai, putting all her concerns behind her, began to think of the undeniable spark between her friends, and she desired nothing more than to fan it into flames. It offered her a chance to witness and perhaps understand the subject of romantic love.

EIGHTEEN

On the evening of Nathan's arrival, Ai sat to dine with the royal siblings. Michael stood behind her, whilst Nathan remained in his allotted bedchamber.

The dinner was a quiet one and the Ore princess dared not look at the sovereign. Since she had not had the opportunity to ponder on his words and actions the previous evening, she hoped to avoid him at all costs.

She ate hurriedly and excused herself. It was with great relief that she bade the royal siblings a good night, and went away with Michael, gladdened the king did not request another private meeting with her.

She asked Michael to lead her to where Nathan was lodged. Her knight raised a questioning brow but did as he was told. Nathan was awake and looked well-rested when he opened the door of the bedchamber to them.

"Nathan, walk with me, for I fear, I am unable to sleep with so many thoughts of my father's indignation plaguing me. I so urgently need to be diverted, and you, my dear friend, are the best person to offer me tales to calm my nerves."

The man gave a sceptical look but agreed to walk with her. "I shall tell you that I am immensely suspicious of your motives, for there is a familiar mischievous look in your eyes. I do not doubt that I am to be your victim." The princess was surprised at how accurate he was in his opinion and wondered if she could achieve what she intended.

"I should have guessed you would be so distrusting and unkind. The only reason you think I am up to no good is because you always contrive to do mischief. Now you can never trust anyone because of your guilt. If you choose to be so provoking, sir, then please take yourself off to bed." Ai said, feigning hurt.

"I do beg your pardon, ma'am. I am at your service. What tales do you desire to know of?"

"Nathan! Do not call me that odious title! You may reserve it for the elderly women of Ore. I must say that you and Michael are cut from the same cloth."

"Alas, princess, I have said nothing to provoke you. Why do you choose to insult me so?" Michael inquired, looking offended.

"Michael! You greenhorn! It is your blessing to be likened to me. I agree with you on that one, Ai. I have sometimes considered that we are very similar..." A slap on his head made him cease from speaking.

"Michael, how odious of you to strike Nathan again, when he has said he might die if you do so. Come and sit Nathan, I shall save you from this brutish man." Ai said laughing, as she gestured to a bench in the large passage. Nathan, holding his assaulted head obeyed silently, and in the next moment, the trio were chatting merrily.

As soon as Ai noticed that Nathan's scepticism towards her was gone, she began to ask questions about his thoughts on the Bamish palace, in comparison to Ore.

"How about the royals? What do you think of them?" She asked.

"Well, I have only interacted with one royal, so I cannot make a complete judgement."

"Well, tell me what your thoughts are. She is a princess and so am I. Perhaps, she appears superior?" Ai pushed.

"I do not think a comparison should be made, but differences should certainly be appreciated. I did not know she was a princess when I entered the room. I expected that the Bamish princess would be ridiculously haughty, especially, with the reputation of her father, but she is the most beautiful creature I ever laid my eyes on. She was also perfectly amiable, and I must confess that I was awestruck by her person."

The princess had never heard her friend speak about anyone the way he did and concluded that they were most certainly infatuated with each other. She acted indifferent to his description and asked about other things to prevent any suspicion of her real purpose. After a short while, she arose.

"I must thank you, dear Nathan, for I am truly diverted." On this note, they parted.

"What in heaven's name are you scheming, princess?" Michael asked as soon as they were away from Nathan and Ai smiled mischievously at him.

"Do not worry your mind about my schemes, Michael. I do however need you to make certain that I am awake at least two hours before noon on the morrow. Then you must send word to Nathan requesting him as my chaperone for a tour around Bamah." When she saw that he was looking at her with evident suspicion, she laughed sheepishly. "It shall be the greatest diversion to see the beautiful towns in this kingdom, shall it not?" She asked as they reached her doors, and went in hurriedly before the Knight could deceive her into spilling the truth.

The next morning, the princess awoke to the loud sound of knocking on her door. She did not feel like being awakened and struggled to rise. Since the sound was persistent, she got off the bed and threw on her robes before going to the doors. She opened it slightly to see her knight standing and regarding her from below his eyes.

"It is now less than two hours before noon. I have been striving to awaken you for several minutes without success."

"Oh dear! If you please, Michael, call for the maids to assist me at once. Have you sent word to Nathan?" She questioned and confirmed that he had done as she bade him the previous night.

The maidservants came in shortly to prepare her for the day, and she sent one of them with an urgent message for their princess. She ate a simple breakfast, and some minutes before noon, she was ready for the day's adventure. She stepped out of her chambers to see her knight waiting at her door, looking ready to be off.

"Now sir, how is it that you are still at my door? I do think you should have this day off."

"If it is a part of your scheme to be rid of me today, I assure you that you have quite failed. If you must know, I allowed other soldiers keep watch of your chambers through the night. You can be assured that I am well rested."

Ai decided within herself to hide her scheme from him as much as she could. She charged him with ensuring that the Ore soldiers took the day to rest. She was glad he did not insist on taking them along, since there was a host of Bamish soldiers accompanying them.

Nathan was awaiting them at her carriage, at the entrance of the palace. He waved at Michael, who was receiving his horse from an Ore soldier and handed the princess up into the carriage.

"Your sudden desire to tour this kingdom is just as suspicious as not telling me about it yesterday!" He said as he sat himself beside her, not bothering with formal greetings.

The princess was too full of excitement, to think of a smart response, so she held her peace. Nathan raised a brow at her as she smiled to herself instead.

"I recognise that smile, and I am most certain that you are up to no good. For the love of God, Ai, would you tell me where we are going?" Nathan said, apprehensively.

"Why, did not Michael tell you?"

"Do not think that I believed, even for a moment that you wish for me to accompany you on a tour. I am not stupid."

"It is my utmost displeasure to disappoint you, sir, for we are indeed going on a tour. Not that I dare to claim that you are stupid." Ai responded sardonically, her grin getting wider. It was the most exciting scheme she had done in all her life.

"Then, what do we wait around for?" Nathan asked, exasperatedly.

"Your impatience shall be the death of you, dear friend. If you must know, it is not what we are waiting for, but who."

Nathan frowned at this. He opened his mouth to speak, but before he had the opportunity, the carriage door flung open and Isa climbed on, helped by a servant.

"Dear Ai, accept my sincere apologies for my tardiness, but it was of utmost importance to make my brother aware of..." Isa's words ceased on her lips as she saw Nathan. Her reaction to his presence caused her to begin to fall back. Ai feared the imminent disaster, but Nathan was up, and able to catch her hand, steadying her.

Their eyes locked for a few moments and Isa sheepishly muttered words of thanks before sitting in the carriage beside Ai. The Ore princess watched the pair in amusement. It was almost as though a scene from a romantic book was played out before her.

After Isa was settled, Nathan gave Ai a knowing look, and she knew he had caught on to her matchmaking scheme. The journey was quite a silent one, with Ai constantly prompting the flustered Bamish royal to tell of the beautiful landmarks they passed. She noticed the two stealing glances at each other and was certain that if they continued in the carriage, her plan would never work.

"Ah, what a beautiful place!" Ai exclaimed as they passed by a vast garden with many kinds of colourful trees and flowers. It was so large that the princess could not see its ends.

"Ah, yes, that is the pride of Bamah, popularly referred to as the gardens of love. I never have had the opportunity to walk in it myself, but I always thought it was so magnificent," Isa responded looking just as awed as the Ore princess who had only read of it in books.

"Shall we stop the carriage and take a walk in it?" Ai asked rhetorically, signalling for the carriage to stop.

Isa cast her a wary glance. "Can we?"

"I do not see why not," Ai responded, with a questioning look. "You are the princess of this kingdom. I do not believe that you could be restricted from entering any public place you choose." Upon reflection of her circumstances, she added, "Except it poses some sort of danger to your life."

Isa looked to be in deep thought. "No, I do not think it is anything of that sort. Only, my father forbade me from visiting such a place that is so much associated with love. He believed that it was the weakest part of the kingdom and always said that love is for the weak."

Ai frowned at her words. She did not know much of the previous Bamish king but that he was the reason the festival of great kingdoms ended. He was consistently losing any form of esteem in her mind. He sounded all too different from her father who encouraged her to live up to her name and love freely.

"What are your sentiments, Princess Isa? Do you truly believe that love is for the weak?" Nathan asked to Ai's surprise. He had been silent throughout the trip in an obvious attempt to frustrate her plans.

"In truth, if love was indeed for the weak, I would rather be weak," Isa replied passionately and blushed when Nathan smiled at her.

Ai grinned widely at the exchange. "Shall we go into the garden then?"

"I do not see why not!" Isa replied excitedly.

NINETEEN

They walked through the seemingly endless, but well-tended field and Ai thought that it was the most beautiful place she had ever beheld. It had several flowers and trees that created unique designs around its walking paths. She considered that replicating it in Ore might be a splendid idea for the lands she had jurisdiction over. Despite its magnificence, she observed with disappointment that the garden was missing the most important thing.

People.

"Why, there is not a single soul in this marvellous place. Does no one in Bamah come here?" She wondered if everyone else in Bamah shared their previous king's sentiments and thought of love as for the weak. It put her in remembrance of Johin's declaration to her and she hoped he did not share his father's judgement on the matter. Before she could dwell on the thought, Isa responded.

"Unfortunately, Ai, I cannot answer that for this is also the first time I have set foot on this field. However, when I think of it, before we shut our borders, it was most assuredly a tourist attraction. It seems to have been abandoned since the end of the Yachad festival."

"Who then tends to the gardens? It does not look at all neglected. It looks affectionately cared for and it is too vast for one or two men to handle."

"Dear Ai, I could not answer you if I wanted to. Perhaps my brother would know better."

"Will he?" Ai questioned warily, as she was again put in mind of Johin's declaration and the true reason she had orchestrated the tour. She began thinking up a way to put her plans in motion and walked silently with the party.

After several minutes of walking deep into the fields in the same direction, Ai suddenly gasped and began frantically searching the pockets of her skirt.

"Oh dear, I think I have dropped my handkerchief," She exclaimed.

"You can have mine," Isa said, offering her delicately seamed handkerchief.

"Alas, I must seek mine, for it was given by my mother and is most dear to me."

"Then, I shall gladly help search for it," Isa said kindly.

"No, you must not!" Ai exclaimed and noticed Nathan's raised brow. She could tell that he was again suspicious of her actions but ignored him. "What I mean, dear Isa, is that I do not wish to ruin your first visit to this wonderful place. I shall leave you in Nathan's care and under the protection of your soldiers. Come now Michael, we shall seek my dear piece of fabric at once." She turned around and walked away briskly, leaving no room for protest.

Ai hummed in excitement as they walked farther away from the group. Although walking through the gardens of love was an unexpected addition to her plans, it contributed a great deal to the potential of her friends becoming infatuated with each other.

"What mischief are you up to this time?" She heard Michael ask from behind her.

She turned to him with a wide smile, unable to cease from grinning. "I do not know what you speak of."

"It is quite apparent that you purposefully dropped your handkerchief." He said dryly.

"It only is obvious to you, Michael, for your perception is almost supernatural. Well, perhaps it was apparent to Nathan as well, for he did not look as though he believed a word I said. Nonetheless, I was not lying when I said I dropped it, I only created a situation. If he again says he is not too stupid to see that I was lying, he shall only be declaring that he is stupid, as he did before we left the palace.

Now, where have I dropped that handkerchief? I must find it, for it truly belongs to Mother," She expressed, looking around frantically.

"Here's the thing. I did see you drop the dear piece of fabric on our fruitless walk and happened to pick it up. I did wonder what your intention was in dropping it." He said, holding out the beautifully patterned fabric.

"My intention is not for you to know. Even if I told you, you would not comprehend it. This might be the one thing that surpasses your superior intelligence." Ai responded, attempting to grab the fabric, but the knight held it high out of her reach, looking unbothered. She gave him a warning look and held out her hand.

"Perhaps I should have said that it was in my possession when you announced that you lost it." He said, putting it in her outstretched hand.

"You would not! I can trust you to always read situations and help me achieve my aim whether you approve or not. You are not like that odious Nathan, who would do all to flout my plans,"

"Princess, you are going in the wrong direction," Michael observed warily as she began to walk down a different path from where she had left her friends.

"I am very much aware of that," Ai replied smugly and continued down the path she was on. She was glad when he did not question her further but silently followed.

As she walked absently down the seemingly endless field, she allowed herself to be lost in her many thoughts. As much as she tried to consider her matchmaking a good deed, deep within, she resisted the guilty feeling that she was doing it more for her benefit than their happiness. She had considered that if Isa and Nathan truly became infatuated, she could witness what it looked like and ascertain if it was the same for herself and the Bamish King.

It was Michael's warning voice, that pulled her from her reflections, but it was rather too late, as she did not observe the obstruction in her path till she tripped over it. She would have fallen on her face, had Michael not caught her by the arm, and steadied her. In an instant, he was standing defensively in front of her.

"What is it, Michael? Did I trip over an animal? Have I hurt it?" she asked, attempting to look beyond his broad figure.

"Please do not hurt me, I do not mean to be out here. I only fell asleep by mistake." she heard the voice of a young boy cry.

Although she was surprised that a child had been sleeping on the ground, nothing prepared her for the shock she felt when Michael gave way. It was a boy who did not seem to have reached the years of adolescence. He was no ordinary child and was the first of his kind she had seen in her existence on earth.

He was a boy with a complexion like hers.

TWENTY

"Please, do not harm me. Forgive me this one time and I shall never make this mistake again." The boy who was sitting on the grass and shuddering in fear pleaded as tears streamed down from his closed eyes.

"There, there, child, fear not. We shall do you no harm. Forgive me for not looking where I was going." Her words seemed to have a calming effect on him, as he ceased shuddering, and slowly opened his eyes. His mouth dropped open at the sight of her, and he fell back in apparent surprise.

"I do not believe I am worthy of such an amusing reaction. Why, do I appear so shocking?" She asked, chuckling.

The boy shook his head. "You are not from my village. I am sure because I know everyone in my village. Who are you and who is this strange man?" He questioned, looking from her to Michael.

Ai laughed at the irony of Michael being referred to as the strange one. "No child, I am certainly not from your village. My name is Ai, and this is Michael." She said gesturing to the knight.

"Ai... What a strange name." The boy expressed thoughtfully.

"That will be Princess Ai to you," Michael interjected, and Ai gave him a sardonic look.

"Now Michael, I do not at all see how that signifies."

"Are you a princess?" The boy asked excitedly, and she turned to see he was looking less frightened and more curious.

"Yes, indeed, I am."

As though prompted, the boy got up abruptly, dusted his clothes, and executed an impressive bow.

"My name is Runo," he said with a wide grin on his face.

"I am pleased to make your acquaintance, Runo," Ai responded, matching his smile.

"Will you come with me to the village? I have told my sister that I shall one day meet a beautiful princess. She would not believe it if I told her I truly did. You must come."

"Then, I must," Ai said, flustered by his words, yet eager to meet anyone else who looked like herself. The idea of a village filled with such people was too good to miss.

"Princess," Michael called in a warning tone. She turned to see his raised brow and could almost imagine what was going through his distrusting mind.

"I am going with him, with, or without you." She said stubbornly, knowing he would never leave her by herself. He frowned at her words but said nothing. "Michael, this might be my only opportunity to meet people who look like me... Please..."

The knight shut his eyes and released a deep breath. "Lead the way, little boy."

Runo led them through several winding paths away from the actual footpaths till they eventually arrived at one end of the garden. It was surrounded by tall hedges of overgrown plants, and they walked through a small opening that could have been easily missed. Ai was reminded of her secret garden back in Ore, and for a short moment, she longed for her home.

That sentiment was immediately forgotten as they walked into the forest on the other side of the garden. At first, it looked like any other forest, but as the boy led them beyond the first set of trees, it became obvious that it was no normal forest, but one designed to keep intruders out. They walked for a while down a tricky path with many twists and turns, till they arrived at a most beautiful little village.

It was so picturesque that the princess had a strong desire to paint it. Houses in the village appeared to be made of wood and clay but were designed most artistically. The village was beautified with trees and flowers, like the garden of love, but better arrayed, with a path leading to a stream.

The streets of the village were very quiet and appeared as though they had been deserted. This did not seem to surprise the boy, who led them into a small house. The inside seemed bigger than it appeared on the outside. There were chairs, a shelf of books, a reading table and everything that made it look like a mix of a drawing room and a library. Two closed doors led to other parts of the house. One of the doors flung open and a young girl walked out.

"You are late again for prayers, Runo. This time, I shall tell Uncle..." She was saying but gasped at the sight of the two strangers.

Ai was in awe of the little girl. She was undeniably beautiful, with skin as dark as hers, big pretty eyes, a tiny nose, and full lips. Ai felt like she had finally found someone in her exact likeness. The girl was attired in a simple long dress, made with what seemed like hand-woven materials, and her hair was intricately braided.

"I told you, Ruona, that I shall one day meet a princess. Look, I have brought one home." Runo said smugly. The girl was so stunned that she kept gasping anytime she attempted to say anything.

Ai, already endeared to the two children was about to introduce herself to the girl, when Michael, with a speed distinct to him, unsheathed his sword and deflected a knife that had been thrown towards her. In the next moment, a sturdy man, only a few inches shorter than Michael jumped into the house and began launching attacks on her knight.

Ai gazed in amazement at the attacker. He was a very handsome, tall man, with a complexion that was darker than hers and fierce dark eyes. He had an air that made him almost as intimidating as Michael.

She was unsure of what to do since the opponent had not stated his reason for attacking. She was however certain from the look on her knight's face that he was not taking the man seriously.

As expected, Michael swiftly switched to launching offensive attacks that caused his opponent to the defensive, till he was forced out of the house.

"Michael, stop this at once!" Ai commanded, following the men out of the house. Even amidst the fight, he was able to turn to her and offer a sour look, as though the princess was bringing his enjoyment to an unnecessary halt. He did as he was told, but not before unarming the valiant man.

"It is quite cruel of you to ask me to stop when you know how rare it is for me to find a formidable opponent, princess."

"This is no place or time for your enjoyment, Michael. You will recall that we are in unfamiliar territory. You should know better than to offend anyone."

"You must also recall that we were attacked first, and I have only retaliated in your defence, your Highness," Michael replied dryly. The princess would have responded but was interrupted by the opponent's deep voice.

"Ruona?" He called to her and Ai gave him a confused look. She remembered that Runo had just called the little girl the same name and wondered if the man was ill in the head. "Ruona." He called again looking desperately into her eyes.

"Uncle, I am here." The little girl answered, stepping out of the house. But the man ignored her, and as though in a daze, he began approaching the princess, calling her the same name. It was only when Michael stretched out his sword to him that he halted.

"Are you not Ruona?" The man asked, and Ai was going to respond in the negative when he spoke again. "No, you could not be. I buried her with my own hands. Who are you? Why are you here?"

At that time several others began to gather around. Ai gazed in fascination at the people who bore different shades of dark complexion. Michael seemed out of place, being the only one with such a bright complexion. Some of the men had their swords out as the knight's was still pointed at his opponent.

"Uncle, this is a princess, and I think the big man is her protector," Runo said stepping into the middle of the exchange. The man frowned looking at her with unhidden suspicion.

"Are you truly a princess?"

"I am indeed," Ai responded calmly.

"Then you must have travelled a mighty long way from Africa into Bamah." He said with much conviction.

"No sir, I have not come from Africa." The man looked at her incredulously, with a raised brow.

"Pray tell ma'am, what princess are you? Be assured that I shall not be as foolish as my nephew to believe your lies. A princess with one man in her defence, ha! What a tale."

Ai frowned with indignation, "I hope to disappoint you, foolish sir, for I am the princess of Ore, and this one man who has so flawlessly defeated you, is worth more than an army in my defence."

She expected the man to doubt her and ask further questions, but to her surprise, he instead appeared stunned by her response. Loud gasps from the villagers made Ai wonder if she had made a wrong decision in disclosing her identity. Michael moved closer to her protectively as though anticipating an attack.

TWENTY-ONE

"You are the dark princess of Ore." The man said looking as though he had suddenly been enlightened. The armed men put their weapons away and the people gazed upon her with awe.

They suddenly began to speak of her praises, and even Ruona gazed at her in open admiration. Ai did not know what to make of their change of attitude.

"Before now, we have only heard and read of you. A princess with skin like ours, ruling over the ones who believe their complexion is superior. I began to believe you were only a fable." An older woman said aloud.

"I did not believe it when we heard the tales, many years ago that the Ore king had adopted a dark babe. But you are here, in the flesh." An older man said, and many others shared similar thoughts.

The princess suddenly felt unworthy of the praises that she had done nothing to deserve. She began to inwardly reflect that if she received the same honour in Ore, it would feel well deserved. She had spent her life toiling in royal duties to receive even the slightest show of acceptance from her people.

"If you truly are the princess of Ore, what business do you have in these parts? Have you come to seek the favour of the new king? Perhaps, to offer yourself in marriage." The burly man who had attacked them earlier said scornfully. He seemed to be the only one who was not awed by her identity.

"Neither! I am a guest of the king of Bamah and contrary to your assumptions, he has sought to court me and has requested my presence here as some sort of diplomatic visit." Ai explained and the people began to murmur in their strange language. The man, however, seemed more relaxed at her response.

"This is my uncle Marho, and he is very protective of the village," Runo explained, pointing to the man, who ignored him and attempted in futility to dismiss the curious crowds.

"You must pardon my harsh manners, princess. I have no grudges against the new king, but we cannot be too careful to protect our little clan. Our secret trading with Bamah has helped us live in peace for many years. Perhaps our lives shall be better if the king does wed someone who looks like us." Marho said and led them into the house they had been earlier.

"What is this trading you speak of, and why do you not live amongst the people of Bamah?" Ai asked, with evident curiosity as she sat on the wooden bench provided for her. Micheal opted to stand, whilst Marho and the children sat on benches as well.

The man who seemed to have become more trusting towards her, told her how his clan, came from a long line of people forcefully removed from western Africa and sold to slave traders in Europe, some were eventually freed, and others fled their brutish masters. They called themselves the Akpor clan and migrated as a group through mountains and seas, till they found a beautiful land where they settled.

They lived independently for many years, growing crops and gardens, till the gardens of love were created. News reached the clan that the kingdom of Bamah had begun expanding its lands by conquering territories. When it was apparent that they were a part of the lands that Bamah wished to conquer, the then leader of the clan approached the Bamish King, who signed a peace agreement with them. At the time the Bamish people were allowed to freely roam the fields and even the King and his wife would always visit their lands.

However, when that king died and his son took over, he desired to conquer all the lands his father did not. He put the clan under siege and took over the garden, making it a tourist location from which Bamah could get revenue. It was soon realised that the beautiful field began to wither for lack of sufficient care, as nothing his people did could sustain it. The secrets of its sustenance were known only to the Akpor people.

That king sought to put the clan to forced labour but soon realised that they would rather choose death than return to enslavement. He made a difficult decision to get into an agreement that granted them their independence if they tended to the garden, which had at the time become recognised as Bamah's territory. The leaders of the clan thought it was a good agreement since they had their independent little village and lived in peace.

When that king died, the new King, Bethenel, did not care for the field. He again wanted to take charge of their little territory. His advisors, however, counselled against it, knowing the good fight the people put against the previous king.

Since they only knew how to take care of the gardens which made Bamah a renowned attraction to people all over the world, the king reluctantly agreed to it. He however put a clause to the agreement, allowing the clan to only work in the gardens on agreed days of trade. Outside these times grave consequences awaited any who broke the agreement.

When Bamah closed itself off from the world, after the defunct festival of great kingdoms, the people of the clan realised that they had nothing to hold against the kingdom. Since the garden was no longer a tourist destination, they were at risk of being conquered and becoming enslaved. They therefore turned to

God, Whom their ancestors had come to know and serve since the times of their slavery, for their protection. A daily prayer hour was created, where all ceased from their engagements to pray to remain in safety.

Being a small clan, they could have been easily conquered by the Bamish army, but somehow, King Bethenel did not besiege them for many years. It was almost as though he forgot of their existence. The people believed that the Most High had heard them and made him forget. However, one day, they unexpectedly received an ultimatum to willingly submit themselves to Bamah or be coerced into submission. The king was travelling overseas and expected to have their little territory and their people, on his return.

The clan intensified their prayers and to their amazement, the king never returned, as he died at sea. The prayer hour then became a tradition for them, as they believed it was what delivered them from the hardened king. They kept the field in perfect condition and still operated their trading with Bamah as normal.

Ai listened carefully as Marho spoke. She was not surprised about the previous King's behaviour, since she had no good opinion of him since he put an end to the festival.

"When King Johin ascended the throne, what did he do?" She asked, eager to know the heart of the man she was courting.

"He did nothing. We believe that he knows little or nothing of our clan. However, he has only been on the throne for over a year, we do not expect that he will become familiar with all that his father intended, nor do we know if he is as cruel as his father. Perhaps it is in our favour that he has chosen to court someone who has the same complexion as our clan." The man replied in a hopeful tone.

"Why did you believe the princess was called Ruona" Michael suddenly asked. It was out of character for him to cut into a conversation, and Ai knew that he was being calculative of all that had happened since they arrived at the village. Marho suddenly seemed flustered by the question, as he looked cautiously at the two children in the room.

He was happily spared from having to respond when a most beautiful woman, walked into the house and sat beside him. She looked ethereal with big lovely dark eyes, full brown lips, smooth umber brown skin and dark hair braided in magnificent rows atop her head. As she spoke the clan's language in a singsong voice, dimples could be seen on both sides of her high cheekbones. Ai gazed at her in awe, but only received a look of contempt in return.

"This is Nana, my betrothed," Marho explained, as the woman possessively put her arm through his. Ai, although surprised at her hostile manner, offered a small smile, but was again met with the woman's glaring eyes. "She has come to ask if you would like to have a meal together with the villagers."

Ai turned to Michael with hopeful eyes, as she wondered what delicacies the clan offered. She was met with a look that made her sigh. "Unfortunately, sir, we must decline your kind offer, as I have left my friends in the field for long enough. I do not wish to have a search party after me." Ai responded, rising, and Marho nodded doing the same.

"I have wronged you in my initial judgement. Please accept my sincere apologies. I see you are quite virtuous and humble, and unlike any royal I have been privileged to meet."

"You flatter me, sir. I have done nothing beyond what is normal. I shall take my leave of you and your wonderful clan."

Marho offered to lead them back to the love gardens but was refused by Michael. The princess said her goodbyes to the children and the man, offering her gratitude for their hospitality, and assuring them of her Knight's superior sense of direction.

She walked in comfortable silence beside Michael who easily led them back to the entrance of the field where the carriages were. Ai was rueful of her hurried return, since neither of her friends was anywhere in sight.

They were forced to wait for almost an hour before Isa and Nathan were seen. The oblivious couple walked arm in arm at a slow pace, lost in a world of their own making. Ai alighted the carriage where she had sat waiting and stood with her arms folded. Isa was the first to spot her and immediately pulled her hand out of Nathan's.

"My dear Ai, why on earth did you not return to us?" she questioned, in an unsuccessful attempt to conceal her embarrassment.

"It appears that you neither noticed nor missed my absence," Ai responded, causing her friend to blush.

"I presumed you would return and..." Isa began explaining, but Ai raised her hand to stop her.

"I am neither offended nor troubled by your delay, my dear friend. Do let us venture on and cover as many sights as we can."

This was done without further ado, and Isa soon lost her blush as she showed Ai the various sights in the city, explaining that it was only a small part of Bamah, since the kingdom had many cities and villages. Nathan acknowledged that whilst it was like Ore in many ways, it seemed bigger and more magnificent. It was almost dusk when they decided to return to the palace.

Dinner was served in a smaller room than usual, and Ai felt more comfortable out of the watchful eye of Johin. "Tonight, shall we eat as friends?" she asked, turning to Michael, who was standing behind her. He regarded her for a moment, and Ai was almost certain he would say something formal and refuse on Isa's account. To her surprise, he simply nodded and took a seat beside her.

"Since you are the oldest amongst us, you should say a blessing over the meal, ancient one?" Nathan proposed grinning widely at Michael.

"I am certain your father would be very proud to see you avoiding priestly responsibilities, puppy," Michael responded sardonically, but his words were brushed off with a shrug. He did as he was asked, and the four ate in comfortable silence. After dinner, Isa led them to a small drawing room, which seemed homier than every other room in the large palace.

There, they sat and began to speak and jest with each other. Nathan and Ai took turns in telling embarrassing tales about themselves and Michael only spoke sarcastic comments that disfavoured Nathan. At the end of the evening, it was clear that Nathan and Isa had mutual admiration for each other.

Ai revelled in the moments she had without the formality of ranks or considerations of appearance. She wondered what had happened in the gardens that had made her friends so openly endeared towards each other and pondered the possibility of achieving the same with Johin.

After dinner, the two princesses took a walk in the garden, followed closely by Michael, whilst Nathan retired for the night.

"How was your time with Nathan, dear friend?" Ai asked, curiously smirking at Isa.

Isa gasped and turned to gaze at her. "Nathan was right. It was all a part of your mischievous plan."

"Well, Nathan and I have been friends for so many years. It is no surprise that he discovered my scheme." Ai responded, smiling nonchalantly.

"Oh Ai, I am so terrified." These words had the effect of bringing the Ore princess to a halt.

"Why Isa? Did Nathan say something foolish? I admit that he can be quite tiresome, but I can assure you that he would never purposefully do anything hurtful. I should not have left you alone in his company if I thought otherwise."

"No, no, dear Ai, it is nothing of that sort, I assure you. On the contrary, I am afraid I might be in love with Nathan." Ai's jaw dropped, as she stood looking dazed and speechless at her friend's unexpected confession. "Please do not say it is too soon to tell, for I am quite certain of my heart and have never felt this way about anyone in my life. I have met very beautiful men in the past who have caught my fancy, but none compares to Nathan. He is different to all. Perhaps, it is the semblance he bears to the teacher who I fancied myself in love with as a child, that has made it so easy for my heart to be set on him. Nonetheless, I am convinced without doubt that I am in love, and I shall have no other but him."

Ai found that she was unable to think of a sufficient response. She had hoped they would have left Bamah before Isa and Nathan became seriously entangled in a relationship that was doomed to fail.

"But how can you tell?" Ai questioned wearily, almost feeling faint as she considered the large gap in their statuses.

"Oh Ai," Isa said, staring dreamily into space. "I cannot stop thinking about him. When we were together in the field, it felt like nothing else existed. Even at this moment, I dearly long to be with him. How I long for this night to end, so I may see him again in the day."

Ai breathed shakily and offered a forced smile. She had known something could become of the infatuation her friends shared, but she did not expect it to occur so swiftly. The books she had read spoke of people being infatuated and getting over it with time and distance. Love, however, was a different matter.

Perhaps it is the way of the Bamish to fall in love so quickly. She thought, considering Johin's confession.

After some time of listening to Isa express her feelings in detail, they bid each other good night. Ai went to see Nathan, in the hope that he did not share Isa's strong feelings. Her usually confident friend, however, seemed like a different person at the mention of the Bamish princess.

"Has she said anything about me? Ai, could you ask your father to bestow me with a title, so I may be worthy of her hand."

"Please, Nathan, do not tell me that you have fallen in love with Isa," Ai said bluntly, taken aback by his earnest expression.

Nathan regarded her with a frown. "Would it be so abominable if I did? I could have sworn it was what you intended with all your scheming today." He said accusingly.

TWENTY-TWO

Late afternoon the next day, Ai decided to walk around the Bamish palace, hoping to clear her mind of the thoughts that plagued her.

The impossible love of Nathan and Isa.

Although she had schemed to see something between them, she was put in mind of the consequences of their being together. She did not think the people of Bamah would willingly allow their princess to wed an adopted son of a prophet, regardless of the nobility of his deceased parents.

On her way back to her chambers, she was again brought to an alarming distress, when she saw Isa sitting with Nathan in one of the palace gardens. They were speaking, laughing, and gazing upon each other in apparent adoration. They seemed to be in ignorant bliss about the hopelessness of their circumstance.

"I would have supposed this was your desire, after all you did yesterday. The look on your face at this moment, makes me question my judgement." Michael said as he stood beside her and observed the couple.

"Hush, Michael. They might hear you!" She said, swiftly walking on towards her chambers.

Although the reason for her scheming was to observe the process of love, she was shocked at the incredible speed with which it had happened between her friends. It made her rethink her courtship with Johin since it was certain that she felt nothing like what Isa had described. She did not find herself unable to stop thinking about him, nor did she long desperately for his presence.

As they got to the doors of her chambers, she turned to the knight, with a question in her eyes.

"Do you think I am foolish, Michael?"

"I will not go so far as to call you foolish, but I must say that you have made several questionable decisions since we have left Ore." He responded so bluntly that the princess was taken aback.

"If you questioned my decisions, why have you not advised against them." She asked indignantly.

"Perhaps, if you told me of your schemes before acting on them, I would have had the privilege of offering a different perspective." Ai breathed heavily, unable to find any smart response. "Why, did you suddenly realise that you are in love with Nathan and do not wish to give him to another?"

The princess looked at him incredulously. "Michael! Have you some worms in your head?"

"I jest, princess. Forgive me." He said smiling.

"Well, I am not amused, and I am quite out of patience with you." She said and stormed into her chambers.

She spent the rest of the evening trying to rethink her purpose in being in Bamah. She did not know if she could find what she had hoped to find in Bamah.

Love, acceptance...

She took out the small-sized version of the Holy book that Nathan had gifted her on her birthday, thankful she had taken it with her, and turned the pages, till she reached a part of it that she knew all too well but desired a better understanding of.

Love suffers long and is kind; love does not envy; love does not parade itself, is not puffed up; does not behave rudely, does not seek its own, is not provoked, thinks no evil; does not rejoice in iniquity, but rejoices in the truth; bears all things, believes all things, hopes all things, endures all things.

Michael had once debated this part of the Holy Book with her when he was recovering from the orphanage attack. He had, at the time, believed that such love did not exist and had questioned its credibility. Ai recalled vehemently defending what she read, as Prophet Asher had taught her. She had told him, that the Holy Book did not lie, and that her parents were a living example of such love.

Michael is now an embodiment of this love he once claimed did not exist.

She thought retrospectively that she had not fully understood what love was at the time, but on further reflection, she came to realise that Michael, who scoffed at the words of the book, was living it out in service to her. She knew he had studied it many times after he survived the orphanage incident and wondered if he was simply living it out or if he felt...

Ai shook her head to rid herself of the thought. Michael was only doing his duty as her knight and even though he was living out the description of love, it did not signify in her present circumstance.

She fixed her mind on Johin and decided she did not know enough about him to make an informed judgement.

The next morning, she awoke to the sound of heavy banging on her door. She arose abruptly and put on her robe.

"Enter!" She called, and it opened to Michael who looked down at her with a frown.

"One more minute, and I would have broken the doors."

"That would have been rather unnecessary, seeing that the doors are unlocked," Ai observed, dryly. "Why, what is amiss?" She asked, noting the look of concern on his face.

"I would ask you the same, princess. It is long past noon, and you have yet to leave your chambers." He responded with a raised brow.

"Past noon?" The princess questioned, feeling confounded. Try as she may, she just could not understand why she continued to sleep so deeply. At first, she had attributed it to weariness, but she had no reason to feel weary, save her journey to Bamah. In Ore, even when she was exhausted, she still arose with the sun, and other times, earlier.

"Well, the Bamish King sent a servant requesting your presence, several minutes ago... or was it some hours ago?" Michael said nonchalantly.

"Michael! Why did you not wake me?" The princess exclaimed.

"I did not see the urgency of the summons and felt no need to disturb the peace of your slumber. However, after it was past noon, I began to fear you were dead, or dying…"

"How can you be so provoking? I must be dead, or dying before it is proper to awaken…" She stopped, as she struggled to suppress the mirth that threatened to overcome her. "I wonder if I can put my feet on the ground with a knight like you."

In less than an hour, Ai was prepared, putting on her most flattering dress. She was compelled to style her hair herself when the maidservants did a poor job of it. Her sole purpose for that day was to attempt to build love between herself and the Bamish King, and she intended to do all to see that it was achieved.

She was led to the magnificent throne room which seemed to be designed with only gold and precious stones. Her gaze shifted from the perfect architecture of the room to the people in it. Several men, glamorously attired in noble robes stood smiling as she walked into the room. They bowed reverentially, as though she was their princess, and Ai felt a swelling in her chest, as she desired such a willing reception from her people and not the forced reverence she was used to in Ore.

Johin rose as she approached him and regarded her with a smile. "My beloved Ai, you look radiant this fine afternoon." He declared loudly, taking her hand, and holding it to his lips. The princess suddenly became self-conscious, aware that she was the centre of attention, and reflexively pulled her hand from his. The king seemed unbothered by this, as he looked beyond her and addressed the men in the room. "My distinguished noble men, behold the princess of the Ore kingdom, and the one I hope to wed and make your future queen!"

Ai went cold at his words. She understood that their courtship was in the hopes that they would eventually be wed, but hearing the king declare it aloud to his council was beyond alarming. To her utmost surprise, she heard cheers and murmurs of agreement that compelled her to turn to the council.

The men's faces were welcoming and almost full of joy at the prospect of her becoming their queen. Ai had never experienced such reception amongst nobles and found herself relishing their acceptance.

"If you have no objections, I shall have you accompany me to a place I consider most beautiful." Ai found that she had suddenly begun liking the idea of a marriage that would afford her such unforced, reverential, and lauding deference.

She allowed herself to be led out of the room, and the men again bowed low and regarded her with honour. It was contrary to what she experienced in her kingdom, and she did not wish for it to end.

She felt assured that with Johin, she would never have to worry about acceptance and honour. Her people would also realise that she was not the worthless adoptive princess they scorned, but one capable of capturing the heart of such a beautiful and powerful king.

TWENTY-THREE

Ai rode in a carriage for almost an hour to the said location. The first thing she noticed as soon as Micheal helped her alight the carriage was the sounds of water crashing into the earth.

Johin led her through a large forest, and after several moments of walking, they arrived at a clearing. Ai gasped, as she beheld the beauty before her. There was a mighty waterfall and a wide river beyond the clearing. Although she had never seen a waterfall, she had read of and seen paintings of a few of them in farther cities of the western Ore. Her father never gave her leave to visit and nothing could prevail on her mother to persuade him to do so.

"This is so magnificent, Johin. Words fail me." She expressed, in apparent awe and wonder.

"I am pleased it is to your liking. I thought you would appreciate it, for I was told that you thought that an ordinary garden was special." Ai strongly desired to inform him that there was nothing ordinary about the Garden of Love, especially since it was built by a clan of people who looked like herself. She however held her tongue and allowed him to lead her to sit at a table that had been set for them.

She was so enamoured by the waterfall and did not realise the king had been speaking to her, till he took hold of her hands, causing her to jump involuntarily.

"Forgive me Ai, it was not my intention to startle you, but I noticed you were not attending to my words." He explained but did not remove his hand. Ai resisted the urge to retrieve her hand as she recalled that she hoped to achieve love with the king. She looked into his eyes and saw they were intently fixed on her.

"It is of no consequence, Johin. I should offer my apologies, for I was quite distracted by this glorious view before me. I hope to paint it from memory when I arrive in Ore."

"Why must you return to Ore to do so? Ai, you must know that despite the magnificence of this gift nature has offered us, it wanes in the light of your presence. I am enthralled by your beauty, elegance, and wit. I must confess that I have met none like you. You reduce me, the great king of Bamah, the strongest in the world, to a mere man, utterly stricken with love. I have no doubts that I would conquer kingdoms and destroy the earth for you. I am at your mercy, my love."

Ai shifted uncomfortably as the king made bold declarations. Since he was the first man she was courting, she was unaccustomed to his words and did not know how to respond.

Although she had hoped to be able to respond positively to his next declaration, she did not feel like she was ready to. In truth, her main concern at that moment was how embarrassing it was that Michael was within hearing distance.

"Why?" She asked absently, before realising in deeper embarrassment that she had asked a question she should not have. Fortunately, the king did not seem to mind the question.

"I do not know why, nor do I contrive to discover it, but of this one thing I am certain, that there is no one else in this world that I shall want for a wife and queen. I have been around the world and met many women. One unquestionable thing is that since we were children, you have had my heart. Your kindness, gentleness of spirit, frankness and beauty are only a few of the many qualities that endeared you to me. Even as a youth who knew little about love, my heart, my soul, and even my body longed for you."

The princess released the breath she had been unconsciously holding in. Such a confession was what she had read in books on love between a man and a woman. She had long perished the idea of ever experiencing such love. However, beyond all odds, such love was being professed to her by a man so handsome and powerful, who could change her life forever, yet she felt nothing in return.

"Ai?" Johin called softly.

"Forgive me, Johin, but I still do not know what love is, and I remain unable to make such bold declarations. However, I want to try…"

"That is enough for me." Johin interrupted, pulling her hand to his chest. Ai shifted uncomfortably, wondering what Michael thought of them. "I planned this day in the hope that I could make you understand your feelings for me."

Ai frowned. "What do you mean when you say, my feelings for you?" She questioned, unable to conceive the ridiculous notion.

"Yes, beloved. You are just as much in love with me, as I am with you. How could you not be? You do not know it just yet, because you have not had the opportunity to experience the love between a man and a woman. Perhaps if you allow me to show you what it means…" His soft voice faded, and he let his fingers trail up her arm.

Ai reflexively withdrew her arm, as she stared at the king in wide-eyed amazement, but he smirked mischievously at her.

"This, beloved, is what I speak of when I say, you do not know what you feel. The sensations are foreign to you, but I am quite patient and willing to teach you all."

The princess found that she was unable to speak, as her mind was filled with chaotic thoughts. She wondered if he did not know that his actions could make anyone feel dreadfully uncomfortable.

"Shall we eat then?" The king asked, signalling to the servants to serve them. His tone was different from the alluring one he had used a moment ago.

Ai sat in a daze as he ensured they were served choice dishes. She decided to abandon her plans to build love between them since Johin was more experienced and was in great control of the situation.

They ate in silence, and Ai stole a glance at her knight and saw that his gaze was fixed on her, with even more intensity than Johin's. Somehow, she drew comfort in his piercing eyes, knowing he was watching over her, and she was not alone.

Johin had commanded that the soldiers stay at a distance, and all but Michael had obeyed. Fortunately, the king did not say anything about this but took to ignoring him instead.

"May we go closer to the fall?" Johin asked, offering his hand as soon as they were finished with the meal. The princess looked warily at the heavy waves. "You can be assured I shall not let you fall to harm." The sovereign added smiling kindly, and Ai wondered at how different he seemed from when he spoke before their meal. She nodded and put her hand in his, allowing him to lead her to the bank of the river.

He released her hand and dipped his hands in the water. The princess raised a questioning brow at him, and in the next moment, she felt the splash of water hit her face. At first, she stood dazed, unable to believe what had just happened, but was induced to retaliate, as another splash hit her face again.

"Very undignified behaviour from a princess," Johin said laughing, as he dodged the water she threw.

"Heavy words from a sovereign who began such a disagreeable game. Surely you did not begin an assault and expect no retaliation." She said and threw the water in her hands towards him. To her annoyance, he again avoided it easily.

Ai frowned and walked back towards the table, returning with a bowl which once contained fruits. The king watched her with confusion etched on his face. She dipped the bowl in the water, and in the next moment, he was drenched.

Johin stood with his jaw dropped, whilst Ai stared at him, smirking in victory. He recovered quickly and attempted to seize the bowl, but she pulled it out of his reach and threw it as far as she could. They laughed at this and continued splashing and laughing in the shallow part of the water.

"It shall give me great pleasure to spend many days like this with you, Ai," Johin said as they walked back to the carriages, drenched in water.

"It was indeed a wonderful day. It reminded me of the time we spent as children in my secret garden."

The Bamish king took her hand and kissed the back of it. This time she did not tense up or withdraw it. Instead, she smiled, feeling a lot more comfortable in his presence.

By the time they arrived at the palace, they were still drenched, and the servants looked curiously at them, but none dared to ask any questions. Before they separated, Johin turned to Ai and held her hands.

"This has been the best day of my life, and I look forward to spending many like this with you, my beloved." He said and bent to kiss her forehead. The princess reflexively froze at his proximity but did not pull away. Johin slowly withdrew, bidding her goodnight before walking away.

Too embarrassed to look at her knight, she hurried towards her chambers, asking for servants to help her change out of her wet clothes. Struck by a mix of confusing emotions, she decided that there was one person whom she could speak to about her feelings.

As soon as she was in dry clothing, she scurried out of her chambers, and without sparing her knight a glance she went to

Isa's. Michael followed behind but did not attempt to enter the large room when the princess was granted entry. Ai sighed in relief at this, as she did not put it past him to suspect danger behind the princess's doors.

"What's amiss, dear Ai?" her friend asked in a worried tone, as the Ore princess sat with her on one of the exquisite chairs in the room.

"Nothing is amiss, dear friend. There are however a few things that I do not understand and need your counsel for." She whispered, conscious that her knight was on the other side of the door. Isa, seeing her concern, pulled her into an inner chamber that had a desk and several chairs.

Ai, feeling comfortable in the privacy of the room, decided to entrust Isa with her thoughts. She was certain she would expire from inner weariness if she did not share her overwhelming contemplations.

She told the Bamish princess of her initial plans to fall in love with Johin, the king's actions at the waterfall, and his opinion about her feelings. She admitted that she did not feel what Isa claimed to feel about Nathan, and explained that her feelings towards the Bamish King were no different from what she felt towards Isa.

"It amazes me greatly, that you remain unaffected by my brother's charms, for he is quite a shocking flirt. He is rumoured to have the charm that leaves every female falling at his feet. One thing I can assure you, however, is that he has never fixed his attention on anyone as he has with you."

"But why he has, I may never understand, for I daresay, I have done nothing out of the ordinary, neither are my features outstanding."

"On that matter, I shall never be in one accord with you, for your beauty is ethereal. Please do not say your complexion makes you any less beautiful, for it is your very advantage. I have heard from other kingdoms that you are referred to as an exotic beauty. You are everything out of the ordinary and I shall be out of all patience with you if you dare speak of yourself as commonplace." The Bamish princess spoke with such a passion that left Ai feeling flustered and astounded.

She had never heard anyone describe her as Isa did and was tempted to believe her every word. The memory of the disapproving and disdainful looks of her people, and the rumour that had spread of her at her ball, made it so difficult to believe.

"Perhaps it is because you are different, that my brother has formed a lasting passion for you. I do not speak only of your complexion, but all else. You are not like other princesses, for you are kind, considerate and a friend to those who are not your equals. Perhaps it is because you are my brother's first love and you have blossomed to be even better than you were in the past, or perhaps..."

"Isa, please, no more of your assumptions, for his reasons are of little consequence in comparison to the fix I find myself in. I do not, for the life of me, know how I shall contrive to love him as he claims I do."

"I would never have thought it possible for any female to struggle to develop feelings for my poor brother." She said laughing, but ceased when she noticed Ai did not share in her amusement. "Could it be, dear Ai, that your affections are already engaged? That must be it, for I am convinced that Ore is filled with the most beautiful men. It is no surprise that my brother's charms mean little to you."

Ai's brows dipped, as she thought about the princess's words, then shook her head vehemently, as an unexpected image flashed through her mind. "I do not believe my affections are engaged, for I have not set my attention on any eligible bachelor in the past."

"Then you must forgive me, Ai, for I do not have the least notion of what you might do. Perhaps, if you fix your mind on it long enough, you shall come to love my brother. I am certain you will deal greatly together. Oh, what pleasure it shall be to have you as my sister and queen!"

As much as she wished it, she knew nothing she fixed her mind on was sufficient to awaken such feelings towards the king. She was in truth, distracted by the image of Michael's green eyes which had flashed in her mind when Isa asked if her affections were engaged. She concluded that because he was constantly in her presence, he was consuming her mind.

She decided that if she spent several days in Johin's presence like they did earlier that day, he might also consume her thoughts, and she would eventually be able to develop feelings of love for him.

She bade her royal friend goodnight, and left the room, walking towards her chambers. She did not say a word to her knight and wished she could make him go away, so she could focus on Johin.

She was so deep in thought, and oblivious to her surroundings, that she didn't see people approach her till Michael stepped defensively in front of her.

She looked beyond him and beheld a young noble-looking woman with her maidservant and two soldiers in uniforms she did not recognise.

TWENTY-FOUR

Ai observed the woman who walked slowly towards them. Her face was painted and powdered in such a manner that made her appear translucent in the lamp's light. Her golden hair was braided in the most glamorous way and adorned with many shiny jewels. Her dress was so low cut, that Ai thought her bosom would be exposed at any moment.

The woman gazed at Michael like he was some work of art before turning to look at the Ore princess with a frown that made her powdered face appear stiff. Ai would have laughed if she had not been plagued with thoughts that caused her great distress. She simply raised a brow at the woman, awaiting an explanation for the obstruction of her path.

"Ha! It is just as they say, the rumoured dark princess is indeed in Bamah." The lady said condescendingly.

Ai stepped forward from behind Michael. "Are we acquainted?" She asked, unmoved by the woman's futile attempt at intimidation.

"I am Princess Rizera of Novar, one of the most powerful kingdoms of the world, known only..."

"What business do you have with me?" Ai interrupted, unwilling to listen to the boastful accolades the woman was professing.

"Of course, it is expected that you should be without manners. I have no business with you, but I chose to..." Again, the woman was interrupted.

"Then you must excuse me, for I am weary and must retire for the night." Ai began walking away. She had condoned the Ore nobles' behaviours towards her because she desired their acceptance but had no tolerance for anyone outside her kingdom who chose to be hostile.

Since she had been openly scorned by foreign royals during the Yachad festival, she had decided to never allow herself to be bullied by anyone from other kingdoms.

"Do you not wish to know why a dignified princess like me is in Bamah?"

"No, I do not," Ai responded and continued walking.

The woman gasped, evidently surprised by her indifference. "I am in Bamah to make an allegiance through a union with the king."

Ai halted, stunned by the unsolicited, but distressing words. She heard the woman laugh mockingly. "I hear that you are also here wishing to court the king. Well, I am here to establish a union, and as of this moment, I am a guest in this kingdom till it is settled.

Ai took a deep breath and turned to her with a smirk. "If that is the case, Rizona, it would seem you have a lot of work to do. Please accept my best wishes." With these words, she continued on her way.

"My name is Rizera, you insolent wretch!" The woman yelled in anger, but Ai did not look back

As much as she wished to ignore the words she had just heard, it troubled her deeply, and she did not know what to make of it.

"Princess," Michael's soft voice tore through her despair, and she turned to him, and saw a look of concern on his face. Before he had the opportunity to say anything, a maidservant approached them and curtsied.

"His Majesty has commanded that this be given to you, Your Highness," the woman said handing a sealed letter to her. Ai was thankful for the distraction, as the last thing she needed was to keep looking into the green eyes that were obstructing her plans and thoughts.

She bid the knight goodnight and went into the bedchamber where she broke the seal of the letter.

My dearest beloved,

Words fail me to describe the joy I derived from being with you. I look ahead in the hope that we shall spend the rest of our days as we did today. Although I desire more than anything to be with you, my duties to my kingdom cannot be ignored. I desire greatly for you to rule by my side. Till that day, I shall strive to make this kingdom greater, so you may be the proud queen of a glorious kingdom.

Do not seek me tomorrow, for I shall do all to come to you.

You remain my precious jewel.

Forever yours,

J.

Ai read the letter over and again, hoping in futility to feel something akin to pleasure. However, there was a feeling of repugnance that threatened to overcome her, as she reflected on the words of the foreign princess.

If what she claimed was true, Ai wondered what would become of her courtship with the king. She could not abide the thought of being one of many wives, especially to a man she had not grown to love. Her hopes of making herself love the king seemed to be waning with each passing moment. The idea that she was one of the many he was courting made her wish to return to Ore.

She wondered if her desire for acceptance and the acknowledgement of her people was worth her unhappiness since she would certainly have a sad, loveless marriage if she continued with Johin. She desired what her parents had in their marriage, which was a love between two people that endures forever.

That night, she tried to pray but felt so distant from God. She had been so caught up in all the activities in Bamah, that she had not done anything she usually would in her kingdom. Prophet Asher would no doubt be disappointed when he found out just how she had been living. The feeling of guilt was then added to her storm of tumultuous emotions, and she just wanted the troubled night to end.

She did not know what time she slept, but she awakened to the sound of a disturbance outside her door. She arose from the bed and put on her robe, resisting the temptation to return to sleep. She began to suspect that her drowsiness had something to do with the strong smell of incense.

She walked to the door and pulled it slightly ajar to see the broad back of her knight, obstructing her view. Although Ai could not see her, she heard a woman pleading with her knight to grant her entrance into the room.

"Please, sir, I have forgotten an article of great importance. You must allow me to retrieve it before the princess awakens. I swear to you that your soldiers always let me into her chambers every morning before she awakes." The woman pleaded, oblivious to the fact that the princess was standing in the doorway. Michael turned slightly to the princess and raised a questioning brow.

"Well, Princess, what do you make of this?" He asked, stepping out of the way so that she could see the intruder. She was a middle-aged woman who was strangely attired with what looked like sack clothes adorned with crystals and strange ornaments. There was a startled look on the woman's face as though she did not expect the princess to be awake.

"Who are you and what is it you seek?" Ai suddenly had a premonition that things were about to go from bad to worse for her.

"Do you not speak, woman?" Michael questioned, after several moments of the woman's dazed silence.

"Ahem, Your Highness... " The woman started, as though jolted from a trance. "I am Nodrina, a priestess of the Bamish palaces from the days of King Bethenel."

Ai hoped baselessly that she was a priestess of the Almighty God, but from her clothing and her fetish-looking accessories, she knew the chances of that were slim. She gazed upon her warily and with great misgiving.

"And what is it that you have forgotten in my bedchamber, Nodrina?"

"If you would allow me, Your Highness, I shall just take hold of it and leave." The woman said with apparent discomfiture. Ai nodded and gave way to the woman, ignoring Michael's questioning gaze.

Nodrina walked briskly into the chambers and towards a table at the far end of the room. She lifted the fabric covering and was about to pick up the items when Ai's voice reverberated in the room.

"Halt!" She commanded in such an authoritative manner that the woman froze. The smell of incense was so overpowering that she felt as though she would swoon. She was quite certain that it was the same incense that had made her sleep so deeply.

"Step aside," she ordered, coming up from behind the woman, who grudgingly obeyed. The princess bent to look under the table, and nothing could have prepared her for the sight she beheld. She shrieked loudly and took several staggering steps backwards, as she stared bewilderedly at the sight before her.

In the blink of an eye, Michael was in front of her, his sword unsheathed.

TWENTY-FIVE

"What... What is this, woman?" Ai asked shakily, struggling to breathe as her mind swirled at the sight and its implications. She stared with foreboding at the ugly wooden image with two large heads and several hands. It had a single eye at the centre of each head and had no legs. An incense burner, lit with smoking incense was placed in front of it.

"This is herona, your Highness," Nodrina said, with evident fear, as she cast glances at Michael, whose sword remained unsheathed. "It is the god of rest, beauty, fertility, grace, peace and..."

"An Idol?" Ai interrupted, stunned beyond comprehension. She wanted to pinch herself to ascertain that she was not trapped in a horrific dream.

The woman claimed to be a palace priestess, and that would mean, such evil was permitted within Bamah. Ai hoped with all her mind that the woman was an impostor. "How dare you? How dare you bring such an evil thing to me or this palace."

"Princess, I have merely hidden my practice from you because I know that the people of your kingdom have delusions that they serve the so-called Son of the Almighty God. If you think I was not within my rights in this palace, I assure you, that you are mistaken." The woman said, in a sudden burst of confidence. "Our noblemen encouraged my actions, for they wished you could get all the blessings of herona who is most effective for guaranteeing that you birth an heir to the throne. She is not some unseen man that people claim died and resurrected many years ago. This herona is visible, tangible and easily worshipped..."

"You shall worship no graven wood here!" The princess yelled angrily.

"Need I remind you that you are within the Bamish's territories and not your little kingdom? Here in Bamah, we pride ourselves in the liberty we have in our varied methods of worship. We certainly believe in the one Almighty God, the creator, but there are several ways to him, not just this Jesus, your kingdom claim is the only way. If you ask me, you shall be told that it is the reason why we are the greatest..."

"I did not ask, nor do I wish to hear you utter another word from your mouth! Leave, lest I cut off your unruly tongue!"

The woman appeared shaken by the threat and hurriedly attempted to pick up the wooden image, but Ai's loud voice stopped her. "I said leave!" Michael stepped forward, causing Nodrina to back away. She scurried out of the room, and the princess threw the wooden image along with the incense burner into the burning flames of the fireplace.

Ai fell to the ground staring at the ugly carving as it burned. She felt tears well up in her eyes as she thought of the woman's words. She hoped to the heavens that she was a liar and an impostor. Had she been in Ore, she would have had the woman detained, but she was not, she was in a strange territory and knew nothing of their ways or beliefs.

Deep within, the princess knew that it was impossible for an impostor to invade the Bamish palace. Suddenly she was filled with indignation and arose with a resolution in her heart.

"Michael, please guard my doors and permit no one, regardless of their business, to enter these chambers till I am ready to proceed." She stood, with her gaze fixed on the hearth of the fire, as the 'god' became completely engulfed in the flames. She heard the door shut and her mind became fixed on a course of action that brought peace to the raging storms in her heart.

She decided to set her heart right with her Lord. She recalled a part of the Holy Book that Prophet Asher had repeated whenever she had erred or done mischief that she felt guilty about.

'Come boldly, before the throne of grace, that you might obtain mercy.'

She did as he had taught her, kneeling before the unseen but most real throne and repenting of her foolish and selfish choices that led to her present circumstance. She let her tears flow freely, as she prayed and made decisions to make wiser choices that would be more pleasing to her Lord. By the time she arose from the ground, she felt the great peace she did not realise had eluded her since she stepped on Bamah's soil.

With her heart set on all she was to do, she prepared herself for the day, unwilling to be served by any Bamish servant. From all she had read in the past, the kingdoms which had attended the defunct Yachad festival prided in their faithfulness to the only true God.

She had been taught from her childhood to know and serve this God, and it had been her duty as a princess to learn and uphold the precepts and principles of the Holy Book. She had believed it was the same in Bamah and hoped that it was still so because no level of acceptance or love that Johin or his people offered could entice her to indulge in the abominable act of idolatry.

Donning her most comfortable dress and a simple hairstyle, she stepped out to see Michael awaiting her. Although he did not utter a word, his eyes spoke volumes, as he observed her in a manner that was most nostalgic to Ai. It was the same look he had given her at the orphanage when he appeared before her. It assured her of his loyalty unto death.

She headed to the place she knew Johin would be. Although he had clearly stated that she should not seek him that day, she just could not wait till he summoned her. The affair was urgent, and it determined her next course of action.

She passed by a few servants who stopped and bowed to her, and for the first time, she noticed that several of them were wearing necklaces with pendants having the shapes of different graven images.

As she approached the entrance of the Bamish throne room, she saw a tall middle-aged man who looked like a highly placed servant, standing at the doors. He saw her approach and gave a look she was much acquainted with. It was the one with which the nobles of Ore usually regarded her.

"Pardon my rudeness, Your Highness, but I cannot grant you admission to the throne room at this time." He declared haughtily. "The King is in a private meeting along with several noble men and I am under strict orders to deny everyone entry. I shall inform his majesty of your desire to see him, as soon as the meeting is ended."

"Make way, for I am quite determined to see King Johin this moment," Ai spoke calmly, but with an undeniable authority that even the man who had spoken with arrogance faltered.

"Unfortunately, Your Highness, I cannot grant you entry, for no one, not even our dear Princess Isa, is allowed to interfere with such meetings," he responded in an irresolute tone.

"You shall do as the princess says!" Michael ordered in a most intimidating tone that caused the man to shudder and scramble out of the way. The knight pushed open the double doors and she was glad that the Bamish soldiers did nothing to stop him.

She was met with the perplexed faces of the Bamish nobility, and her gaze trailed to the woman that was seated amongst them, her powdered and painted face was most recognisable and even funnier in the daylight.

She shifted her gaze from the woman till it rested on Johin, who was seated on his throne. He leaned forward, as soon as he saw her, with surprise and curiosity, evident on his face. She was hit with the realisation that his meeting with the Novar princess was the reason he had asked her not to seek him.

Ai took a deep breath and began walking towards him. The nobles were so stunned at her audacity that some had their mouths agape. Johin arose as she approached, and the nobles arose with him.

"I do not care that you are a princess of that lowly kingdom. How dare you..." A middle-aged man whom she vaguely recognised, standing beside the throne started, but Ai ignored him and spoke directly to the king.

"I request a private audience at once, King Johin."

At her words, she heard the Novar princess gasp, and murmurs and angry jeers of disapproval soon filled the room.

TWENTY-SIX

Ai stood at the centre of the throne room, unfazed by the noise. She found it amusing that the people who had bowed to her the previous day in what she thought was reverential honour were the same ones saying the worst. She remained calm with her head raised high.

"You insolent..." The middle-aged man started again but stopped when Johin lifted his hand. She recalled where she had seen the man. He was the same man who had introduced the king at her ball.

"Could this not wait, Ai?" Johin asked with a frown.

"No. I must speak with you at once."

She had seen enough to know her stance and was unwilling to remain quiet about it for a moment more. The king's response would determine her next course of action. Her desires and wishes notwithstanding, she would not spare a moment in Bamah if he did confirm all she had discovered.

The noise from the men got louder, some were even uttering curses to her, but she had no fear. She was the princess of Ore and if they dared harm a hair on her head, it meant war between the two nations. Although Ore was smaller than Bamah, it was not a kingdom that could be easily bullied.

"Silence!" Johin yelled out, looking out of patience with the men. The room suddenly became so quiet that a pin would be heard if it was dropped. "Out! Now! Every one of you."

There was a moment of dazed silence among the people, but no one dared to protest. In the next moment, the people began to leave. Johin commanded the servants and soldiers to leave along with the nobles, and they all did so without a word of protest. Ai did not miss the glares and looks of scorn she received from the men. The Novar princess had glared at her with so much hatred, that Ai genuinely thought her face would break in pieces.

She observed that Johin was visibly angered that Michael was the only one who had disobeyed his orders. The knight stood behind her with his arms folded and gaze affixed on the king.

"Please Michael, do give me a few moments," Ai said quickly, as she noticed Johin put a hand on his sword. Although she did not think he could easily defeat Michael, she did not wish to have her knight fighting against a king. The knight glared at Johin one last time, then hesitantly took his leave.

"Oh, how far away I would put this man from you when we are wed, Ai. As far as heaven is from the earth. I do not know why you let him do as he pleases. He is only a mere soldier. Your orders should be absolute, and not a request." Johin said in open agitation, which caused Ai to frown.

"He is not just a mere soldier, but my knight to whom I owe my life, and a friend I trust!".

"I assume you have not sought a private audience to rain praises on that despicable man," Johin stated irritably.

"I did not expect that you would send all your men out for a private audience, having a private meeting in a smaller room would have been sufficient."

"Yes, it might have, but that would be a less thrilling way to show authority." He said walking towards her. "Now tell me, to what do I owe the pleasure of your presence? Others may have found your bold interruption to my meeting insolent and foolhardy, but I found it fiercely intrepid, and alluring. It made my heart soar, and I know we shall deal greatly together. Ruling my kingdom is not for the faint at heart."

He was suddenly too close for Ai's comfort, but she was determined not to back down, even though his smouldering eyes and quiet tone made her want to shrink back.

"Today, a woman by the name, of Nodrina, came into my bedchamber to reclaim a wooden idol she had forgotten. I collect that every morning, whilst I slept, incense was burnt in my assigned bedchambers to this idol. This incense, I perceive, has been the reason I have been unable to awaken early since I arrived in Bamah.

When confronted, the woman boldly said that such worship of graven images is permitted within your kingdom. Naturally, I assumed she was an imposter and cast the wooden image in the fire."

"You cast the image in the fire?" Johin asked in apparent bewilderment. "Ai, you are indeed the most daring woman I have ever met. You must however understand that Bamah prides itself in its liberal ways. Of course, as you know, we royalty are of the Christian faith, but the people you have observed may be of a different religion than ours, and it is within their rights in this kingdom. Whilst I can admit that the service of many gods has sometimes caused rivalry and some problems within the kingdom, I have been assured that it is only a small price to pay for our endless prosperity." He declared, grinning proudly as he reached out for her hand.

Ai immediately pulled back, causing the king's smile to stiffen. She took advantage of the moment and put a good distance between them as she struggled to collect her thoughts. Disappointment and sadness weighed heavily in her heart. The mere thought of marrying into such a confused kingdom filled her with great repugnance.

"From all I thought I knew and learned, all the kingdoms represented at the Yachad festival, served only the Almighty God, not some handmade item that they call a god."

"So much has changed since then, Ai. Even your kingdom was closed off to the world for many years. Bamah prospered by allowing liberality to thrive. Except for a few manageable conflicts, it has increased creativity and productivity among the people. It is why the kingdom continues to flourish, despite its non-alignment with other kingdoms."

"You speak of non-alignment, but I hear there are talks of alignment with the Novar kingdom whose princess I have met. She claims you two shall be wed and an alignment would be formed. Besides, my kingdom has stayed true to its beliefs and has never wanted for creativity or productivity."

"I see what the problem is, my love. Is it the presence of the Novar princess that has put you in a passion? If so, you may rest easy, for I swear to you that she is nothing, but a kingdom to conquer. The nobles of this kingdom have brought her to me with the suggestion that I make a concubine of her. I neither need to wed nor go in with her. However, being that she is the only child of her father, it is an easy way to gain authority over her kingdom. You alone shall be my queen, so we may rule these kingdoms together."

He took a step forward, but Ai only stepped further out of his reach. She looked up at him tearfully, as her emotions threatened to overcome her. The realisation that she also, being a lone princess, would mean submitting her kingdom to his authority if she did wed him, was too hard to bear.

"How is it that you claim to serve the Almighty God, yet you permit your people to commit such grave sins? How can you claim to love me but be attached to other women? What does it matter if I am first amongst others?"

"Even in the Holy book, kings possessed more wives than a great army. King Solomon was the wisest man that ever lived, yet he possessed up to a thousand or more wives and concubines. I, however, offer you a life where you alone are my queen. I need not wed any of these princesses. I shall only make them mistresses to establish alignment with their kingdoms." Johin responded earnestly.

"Lest you forget, the same king you speak of was cursed by God for his abominable worship of idols brought to him by his many women. Even if I chose to overlook the fact that you are considering relations with other women, which I shall not, I could never acquiesce that you intentionally allow your people to worship idols. Have you not read all the things that befell the kings who turned to Idols in the Holy book?"

"I do not worship any idols, Ai. I serve the same God you serve."

"But you allow other gods within your walls and allow your people to freely sin against God. You are king and from my observation, your word is absolute, yet you do not stop them." Ai reasoned, allowing her tears to fall freely down her face.

"Surely, you must understand how people frown, hate and even rebel against us royals when they do not get their desires. How else shall we gain their acceptance? We exist to grant the wishes of the majority. Only then shall they accept us as rulers."

Ai shuddered, as his words hit home. It was the same acceptance she had been seeking when she journeyed to Bamah. She wondered what immoralities lay ahead of the path the Johin had chosen.

TWENTY-SEVEN

Ai gazed sympathetically at the young king. She, more than anyone else, could empathise with his desire to be accepted and how far it could lead, down the wrong path.

"I have come to learn that this acceptance we seek is fickle. Remember, the ones who shouted 'hosanna' to our Lord at one moment, also yelled 'crucify Him' the next. As you have witnessed, I was ridiculed and rejected by the same people who honoured me only a few hours ago. There is only One whose acceptance never changes, and it is He you defy with your principles." She said passionately, hoping he could truly understand her words.

"Bamah has been this way since the end of the Yachad festival. I simply cannot hope to change it because I ascended the throne. What if my kingdom ceases to flourish because of such change? Would not my people turn against me? I am doing my utmost to keep the kingdom as powerful as my father did, hence, I must keep his legacy. I cannot change it." Johin replied as though trying to make her see his reasoning.

Ai took a deep breath and wiped the tears off her face. "I see that your mind is set and nothing I can say can change it, so I will not persist. I shall, however, refuse to ally myself with a kingdom that has turned from the path of our Lord and Saviour, Jesus." She said and watched Johin's facial expression switch to something akin to fear.

"I have not turned away from God, Ai," he started.

"Oh, but you have, King Johin, for there is no middle ground. You are either for the Lord or against Him. You have chosen your path, and now I must choose mine. I am on the Lord's side, and I will not spend another moment in your kingdom. I thank you for your most flattering suit, but I must decline, for I cannot wed you. I wish you happiness with the Novar princess."

"What do you mean by this, Ai?"

"My men and I shall take our leave this moment. I thank you for the hospitality you have granted us during our time in your kingdom." She responded, turning from him and walking towards the doors.

"Ai..." Johin called out softly, as though he wanted to plead with her. When she did not respond and kept walking away, his tone became harsh and autocratic. "You shall remain within Bamah till the date agreed for your departure." His words made the princess halt and look back at him in astonishment.

"I shall do no such thing!" she responded firmly. "You forget yourself, Johin. You are not my king. I am the Princess of Ore and neither I nor my men shall take orders from you or anyone in this kingdom!" She turned again and walked out of the throne room, gladdened he did not follow or physically attempt to stop her.

Michael was waiting outside the room, along with the nobles who had evident curiosity in their eyes. The Novar princess was nowhere in sight, and Ai was thankful, for she did not wish to converse with her.

"Come, Michael, we must take our leave at once." If her words surprised the knight, he did not show it.

"I shall make the arrangements to collect your possessions," he said as they walked.

"There is no need for that, for I must abandon whatever it is I have left in those chambers. We must gather our men and leave this instant." Ai announced, ignoring the surprised murmurs from the nobles, as she walked past them.

They found Nathan sitting in the garden with Isa and they both arose at the sight of her and Michael.

"What's amiss, dear Ai?" Isa questioned, and Ai knew that the look on her face undoubtedly communicated the bad tidings she brought.

"Forgive me, my dear friend, but we must leave this minute," Ai responded, saddened at the prospect of leaving her beloved friend when they had only been reunited for a few days. She was however uncertain if Isa shared her brother's sentiments, and did not wish to discover.

"Oh goodness! What has happened? What has caused you to make such a drastic decision in such a short time? Surely, this was not your resolution after we spoke yesterday. Could it be that one of those wretched nobles has said something to upset you? Please, allow me to set things right." Isa spoke desperately, approaching Ai with tears already springing to her eyes.

"Forgive me, Isa, but I have no time to discuss the matter with you. Your brother might be better suited to explain the situation to you." Isa halted in mid-stride, as her eyes widened.

"My brother? But he adores you and worships the ground you walk on."

"Believe me, that does not at all surprise me," Ai whispered sardonically. She turned to the man who stood back in a daze.

"Come now Nathan, we must leave at once!" The man did as she bid without protest. Although he was her friend, she was also his princess, and her tone was sufficient for him to recognise that she was issuing a royal command.

He stared longingly at Isa as he walked by her, then stopped to kiss her hands, before going with the Ore princess.

"Ai," Isa called again, capturing her attention. "If you must go, then I adjure you, take me with you to your kingdom, that I may dwell with you. I have never known such joy as I have in these few days that you have been in my kingdom. Please, dear friend, do not deny me this."

Ai was disconcerted by her friend's shocking request but recovered almost immediately as she considered the consequences. "As much as I wish to, I cannot allow it, lest it is assumed that you were abducted by my party. I do not wish to stir up an unnecessary war between our kingdoms." She responded and left a sobbing Isa in her wake.

Despite how distraught she was, the Bamish princess ordered servants to provide food supplies for their travels. Ai had been tempted to refuse but knew it would be foolish of her, especially since the journey was long and unplanned. Isa saw to the delivery of these supplies herself, even as Ai and her men prepared to leave. Ai was moved to tears as they departed, wondering if she would ever see her friend again.

She rode in her carriage with Nathan, whilst the rest of her party rode on horseback. It was evening by the time the entourage went past the Bamish borders and Ai was grateful they were not hindered.

"Are you well, Ai?" Nathan asked as they rode across the wilderness outside Bamah. Realising that she had been unconsciously crying, she swiftly wiped her tears, offered him a small smile and nodded.

As soon as they had departed from the palace, she told Nathan her reason for leaving so urgently. Although he had commended her, she noticed the glint of sadness in his eyes. She hoped to beg his pardon for setting up a match that was bound to fail, but before she could utter any words, the carriage came to an abrupt halt. The princess would have been thrown across the coach if Nathan had not reflexively grabbed her shoulders and steadied her.

Ai looked out the window in confusion and observed that they were surrounded by strange men. She opened the carriage door and allowed Nathan to help her out of it. Michael dismounted his horse and took a protective stance in front of her.

In total, she had just thirteen men, including Michael and Nathan. The opposing forces that surrounded them had at least a century of men, and she was certain she would have to defend herself. Although she was quite confident in her swordsmanship, she had never engaged in a real battle.

"What is your purpose and why do you obstruct our path," Ai asked loudly and a man who she assumed to be the leader of the group stepped forward.

"We are here to retrieve you, dark princess. Dead or alive."

TWENTY-EIGHT

Ai stood awestricken, as she slowly grasped the weight of the man's words. In the twinkling of an eye, she was surrounded by the Ore soldiers, who took defensive positions around her, with their swords unsheathed. She did not want to lose any of her men, nor did she want any to die before her since it had taken her too long to recover from the nightmares of the orphanage incident.

"To whom do you wish to take me?" she questioned, hoping to avoid a battle.

"That, I cannot say princess, but you may discover for yourself if you shall be so obliging as to come willingly with us." The man said with a smug smile. Ai considered his words and attempted to step forward, but her guards only tightened their defence around her, surprising her.

"Make way," she commanded but was ignored.

"Only over our corpses shall we allow such a thing to happen," Michael said, and the Ore soldiers muttered words of agreement. Nathan immediately reached into the carriage, grabbed two swords in a storage compartment, handed one to her and spoke.

"Do not for a moment consider offering yourself, Ai. What shall we tell your father if you do? Surely you know that we could not return to Ore with such news. So please let us fight valiantly to the end."

The leader of the opposition yelled a battle cry, and his men responded with an offensive attack. Ai stood clutching the unsheathed sword in her hands for a long time as her men held the defence around her for more than half an hour.

She was surprised at the skill of her soldiers and realised that her father selected Ore's best to go with her. Not one was down and her opponents, being inferior in skill, seemed to rely greatly on their numbers and strategies to keep up.

It was a strategic tactic that allowed for an opening in their defence and a soldier from the opposing army launched an attack against her. To his evident surprise, she easily deflected it. She swiftly knocked the sword out of his hand, leaving him unarmed. Her opponent cowered as though awaiting his death, but Ai stood still, unable to strike. She struggled to breathe at the thought of what was expected of her, as she held a shaky sword to the man.

She had never hurt anyone in her life, and although she was in a kill-or-be-killed dilemma, she just could not bring herself to kill. The soldier, realising this, pulled a dagger out of his pocket. Ai watched limply as he launched at her expecting the worst, but in a split second her vision was cut off by a large hand covering her eyes. She heard the shrieking of a man and knew that her opponent had been put down.

Ai did not need her sight to know it was her knight that had come to her rescue. She felt his other hand gently turn her away from whatever lay before her as he uncovered her eyes. She could see worry evident in his green orbs, as his eyes trailed to her hands. She followed his gaze and realised that she was visibly shuddering.

"Ai," he called, lifting his eyes to hers. "Please, fight. Your life is worth all of ours." Ai nodded, recognising that he had called her by name. She knew it was a dire situation since he rarely ever did and his face held an uncharacteristic expression, as though he feared he could not protect her. He turned away and took on another opponent who was attempting to launch a sneak attack.

Ai looked around and noticed that some of her men were injured. She said a silent prayer for them. Since she had compelled them to leave Bamah, she felt responsible for their predicament. She barely had any time to rethink her actions when the leader of the opposition came up to her, looking ready to strike.

"Here, princess, is where you die."

Ai observed that all her men were overwhelmed with enemy soldiers, and even Michael had his hands full. She saw that it was another tactic to leave her undefended so she could be ambushed. She tightened her grip on the sword in her hand and took a defensive stance. The man raised a brow at this but charged at her. To his evident amazement, she was able to defend against his heavy strikes.

"You are surprisingly skilled for a princess, but you are only a woman. An easy kill." He said and laughed arrogantly.

Ai chose not to respond to his words. He was no doubt a skilled soldier, but she also noticed that he had wronged her in his estimation and took advantage of his ignorance. As soon as she saw an opening, she took the offensive.

Her opponent struggled in vain to take control of the fight, but she gave him no chances, striking swiftly, till she made a move the man could not stave off. She watched as her sword moved towards his neck and grazed it.

The man shut his eyes ready for his end, but the princess froze as a trickle of blood oozed from his broken skin. It was not a deep cut, but it was enough to weaken her resolve. She stood shuddering, unable to complete the deed. The man opened his eyes and smirked, as though comprehending her plight.

"It appears I misjudged your skill, princess. You are a great swordswoman. Nonetheless, your fragile heart shall be the death of you."

Unable to command her body to defend, Ai watched in dismay as the man attempted to strike. Before he had the chance, a sword pierced through his heart from behind him. Her eyes widened in terror as the man fell to the ground and struggled with his last breath.

The princess felt her heart drop, as she saw Johin behind him. There was a frightening coldness in his eyes, as he wiped his bloodied sword on the dying man.

"I watched you battle in such a thrilling manner, but to think you would rather die than kill is beyond all bounds of foolishness."

Ai looked up at him and saw the bloodlust evident in his eyes. She observed that he had about five dozen soldiers behind him and that the enemy soldiers had begun to withdraw.

She assessed the battleground and to her greatest relief, counted her thirteen men including Michael and Nathan. Several were gravely injured but were being attended to by their comrades. She silently offered thanks to the Lord and turned to Johin.

"You shall return with me to my palace, Ai. What great fortune you have that I came after you. Had I chosen not to, you would have been killed. Therefore, I shall see to it that you remain under my watchful care till the agreed date of your departure." He said firmly and turned towards his carriage as though expecting her to follow.

As she watched him, the realisation that he was not the kind boy who followed her to her garden several years before, dawned on her. He was the king of the strongest kingdom she knew, and she was at his mercy.

It was only common sense to return with him, then she could send for a bigger army from Ore. It was foolishness to risk her life and her men, lest they were attacked again on their journey. She wished she had agreed to the hundred men her father had first suggested and wondered about the letter she sent to her grandmother.

"I refuse!" She declared boldly. She had almost resigned to obeying Johin's command when the image of the idol flashed in her mind, and she recalled the reason she had left Bamah in the first place.

She watched as the king ceased walking and turned to her with a deadly glare. As hard as she tried, she could not stop her heart from beating wildly in fear. He began walking towards her.

"What is it you refuse, Ai?" he asked in such an intimidating manner that the princess began taking involuntary steps backwards.

It was as though her body had a mind of its own. She willed herself to stand boldly, but her body trembled in fear. The king halted and Ai noticed a wave of emotions flit across his face.

At first, he seemed surprised at her trembling, then apparent sadness befell him, but it was almost immediately replaced by the coldness she had seen earlier. He resumed walking towards her whilst she kept retreating.

"Tell me, Ai, what is it you are refusing? My help? My protection? My love?" He questioned gesturing with the sword in his hand. Ai opened her mouth to speak, but no words came out of it.

Never in her life had she felt so frightened. Even the orphanage incident could not hold a candle to the horror she felt in that moment.

She was uncertain if it was the image of him killing a man emotionlessly, or simply the thought of being coerced against her will that caused her great trepidation. The one thing she was sure of, was that she did not wish to stay another moment in his presence.

She kept retreating till her back encountered an obstruction. She turned her head to see her knight standing firmly behind her and glaring fiercely at the approaching king.

"The princess has refused you, Bamish king. Regardless of what it means, she shall not be returning with you." Michael said with unconcealed irritation in his voice.

Johin averted his eyes from Ai to her knight and his hatred was almost tangible. "You lowly rat. You dare speak to me in that manner?" He pointed his sword at him, and Michael stepped out from behind Ai.

"Call me what you may, but the princess of Ore shall not be bullied!' Michael declared.

"You are in no position to speak, for I have decided you are no longer worthy to protect my bride. I desire nothing more for a dowry, than your head on a stake."

Michael raised a brow and smirked. "Very quick words, from a man who has just been rejected."

Ai watched in terror as Johin's face contorted in disdain. Running forward, he launched an attack. A fierce battle ensued between the two men, and it was soon evident that Johin was no match for the knight.

The Bamish king was sweating profusely as he struggled to keep up with the knight's attacks. In one moment, he was standing, in the next, he was floored with his sword out of his hand.

His men quickly surrounded Michael whose sword was pointed at Johin. Ai knew that Michael could not harm the king, for the repercussions would be far too great, and it seemed Johin knew it too.

"Cease him!" he yelled angrily and all the Bamish soldiers began to attack, much to Ai's dismay. It was an unfair battle that Michael stood no chance of winning since the Ore soldiers were still occupied with helping the injured.

She decided to charge into the battle and fight beside him but was stopped when a hand reached out and grabbed her arm. She turned to see Nathan with a worried look on his face. It seemed he had predicted her actions.

"Unhand me, Nathan. I must help him!"

"No, Ai, I cannot let you. It is too dangerous! Michael will never forgive me if I do. I must stand in his place and defend you if the need comes." He responded, taking the sword from her before releasing her arm.

Ai frowned but turned again to the battle, afraid for her knight. Somehow, Michael held his ground against the men for several minutes, but at a point, he became open to an assault from the nimble King, who used the force of his leg to send him crashing badly to the ground.

Ai's initial fear that Michael would hit his head on a stone and die, was discarded as she saw him lift himself from the ground, only to be thrown back by another ruthless kick and several blows from the Bamish soldiers. After assaulting the knight numerous times, Johin stood over him with a devilish grin, and the look on his face gave away his intention.

As the king turned to get a sword from his men, her apprehension overcame reasoning, and she ran unarmed towards where her knight lay, deaf to Nathan's protest.

Just as Johin lifted the sword, she threw herself over her knight and shut her eyes, expecting the worst.

TWENTY-NINE

Ai heard the king swear loudly, and it took her a moment to realise that she had not been harmed. She opened her eyes and beheld Johin staring down at her with fear-filled eyes. The tip of his sword was only inches away from her.

"What in the Lord's name are you doing, Ai?" He questioned, throwing his sword away, as though it would harm her of its own volition.

"Stop this now, Johin!" Ai said, feeling her boldness return. She realised that even more than her death, she feared losing Michael. She could see that his eyes were filled with something akin to fright and knew he feared for her life.

After the orphanage incident, he had made her promise to never again attempt to risk her life for him, since she was of greater value to the kingdom. Ai however thought it was an impossible promise since she could not stand by and watch him die.

"You need not kill my knight to make me go with you Johin. You may very well kill me first." She said, unwilling to arise from Michael until she was certain Johin would do him no harm.

"Ai…" She heard Michael's pained voice call.

"Hush, Michael. I know what you wish to say, but I do not want to hear it."

Despite her struggle to hold him down, the knight arose and set her on her feet. Nathan and the Ore soldiers rushed to her side looking ready to battle. Even the injured men were still willing to fight, and Ai was moved by their loyalty. She looked fiercely at the Bamish king, with a challenge in her eyes.

"You would die for this lowly rat?" Johin questioned angrily as he looked from her to her men. Suddenly, he smirked. "Very well, I shall spare your knight on one condition. You shall leave with me and neither he nor your soldiers shall come with us. I give my word that I shall not kill them, but their safety shall not be my responsibility."

"Ai, you must not!" Nathan said desperately, and her men echoed his words.

"But what else shall I do?"

"I shall happily die fighting. Nathan will take you home." Michael responded.

"How foolish of you Michael. You must think your life is worth nothing. I assure you, sir, that you are worth a thousand more than this evil king." She expressed, indignantly, causing Johin to frown again.

"Call me whatever you will, Ai. In time, you shall see that I am doing all because of my love for you."

"You dare call this love? What sort of love forces one against their wishes? Certainly not that which I read in the Holy Book. No Johin, you do not love me. You are so power-obsessed that you cannot stand to be rejected."

The king recoiled at her words and took a step towards her, But Michael and Nathan stepped forward defensively. The Bamish and Ore soldiers also stood alert, as though waiting for instructions to fight.

"How dare you spit on my love like this, Ai? After the Yachad festival, I spent many years longing for the day I would see you. I rejected many betrothal requests in the hope that one day when we meet again, I shall wed you. I spent many years planning how I would make you my princess even if I had to defy my parents.

When I ascended the throne, my first thought was to seek your hand as my queen, even if it met an allegiance with Ore. It was only by good fortune that the love festival brought us together. You do not know the trouble I went through to be at that festival. How dare you question my love for you." The king was breathing heavily in anger by the time he ceased speaking.

"You cannot force a person to love you because you think you love them," Ai responded indignantly. "Did you ever consider that I may not like your arrangements, or have you always planned to use coercive methods?"

"Enough of this nonsense. Come willingly with me, or watch your men perish before you." He responded emotionlessly and Ai could see he meant every word.

The princess considered his demands and realised that he intended to entrap her. Doing as he asked, meant leaving herself and her virtue at his mercy. He could make her his mistress or slave if he so wished. She knew her father would undoubtedly put up a fight to reclaim her, but her virtue would forever be in question.

"I shall go with you," she responded, deciding that all her considerations dimmed in the light of keeping her men alive.

"Now, bid your company goodbye, and come at once to my carriage." He said and turned away from them.

"I shan't allow it" Michael said, obstructing her path. Nathan stood with him and nodded at his words.

"You cannot stop me. This is a royal command!" She said sternly, but he did not move. She looked into his eyes as he gazed at her with sheer determination. "Michael, please, I do not want to lose any of you. Live to fight another day. You and the men may return and inform my father of all that has happened.

"I will rather die than allow you return alone." He insisted, but Ai simply pushed past him and began walking towards the king. "Do you not recall the reason you decided to leave? Has that reason changed because you have been threatened? Do you truly trust the God you claim to serve?" Michael called out causing the princess to halt.

His words hit home, as she recalled that it was not for her selfish desires she was fighting, but for the God whom she believed with all her heart. During her time in Bamah, she had been so self-absorbed and engrossed with being accepted by humans, that she forgot that she was already accepted.

She had also been so consumed by the idea of being loved by a man, that she used human experiments and left broken hearts in the wake of her selfish purposes. For the first time, she was honouring her God and not her selfish desires, yet she was giving up at the first resistance.

Oh Lord, please help me. She cried in her heart as she wiped the tears that were flowing down her face.

"Your majesty, King of Bamah," She called out to him and watched him wince at the formal way she spoke. "I must tell you that I do not wish to go with you. The simple thought of spending a single moment of my time with you is in fact of great repugnance to me. If you do compel me to go with you, I shall not go as the princess of Ore, but as a victim, forced against her wishes to return to a place she holds in utmost aversion."

The king's expression changed from apprehensive surprise to apparent annoyance. "What do you mean by this, Ai?"

"It is just as I say, Your Majesty. Since you have resorted to coercive methods, I shall no longer be your honoured guest, but a prisoner within your walls."

"Do you have no care that I have just saved your life?" He asked, looking agitated.

"You have my sincere gratitude. However, seeing that you almost took the life of my knight, I fear for what my life is worth. I shall go with you, as your prisoner. My father shall then decide on the matter."

The king's expression showed that he understood the implication of her words. If he indeed took the Ore royal as a prisoner, it would be a declaration of war between the two kingdoms. It was Ai's last attempt at disencumbering herself from the clutches of the king.

"How could you, whom I so dearly love, speak with such cruelty?" His voice rose with every word and Ai took a step back, unsure of what to expect from him.

As though noticing her agitation, he took a deep breath and spoke again. "Beloved, do you not see that all I do is for your sake? Your life is in danger. Your attackers could be from any kingdom, yours included. Please, allow me to protect you. Let our love overcome all."

His words pierced her deeper than she could fathom. He was implying that her people hated her enough to kill her, and as much as she wanted to, she could not refute his claim. Johin stretched out his hand towards her, willing her to come to him.

"I refuse." She said firmly, deciding that she would rather return to a people of right standing with God, no matter how much she was scorned. She was afraid but convinced that she would rather die for what she believed than succumb to the life Johin offered.

"Have it your way then!" Johin said angrily, marching towards her. He stopped, as Michael and Nathan took defensive positions in front of her. "I say, you shall return with me, as a prisoner, or as my guest. Even if I had to tie you up or kill your friends, I shall do whatever it takes to have you. Now take my hand and come with me or suffer the consequences of your disobedience."

Oh Lord, help me. Ai cried again within herself. Before she could respond to his threat, the sound of many horses trotting towards them was heard. A Bamish soldier ran up to the king and spoke.

"Your Majesty, we are under attack. No less than a thousand men are approaching."

Ai looked around with dread as she saw the horsemen drawing closer. They had cloaks over their uniform, so she could not tell who they were. She guessed they were reinforcement from her attackers and wondered why it was that she was wanted dead, within and outside her kingdom. Johin swore and instructed his men to prepare for battle. He gave orders for reinforcements from the borders to be brought.

"Come with me Ai, I shall bring you to safety within my borders, my men will hold off the attackers." He said, holding out his hand to her with a glimmer of hope.

Ai turned from him to the fast-approaching army. She decided within herself that she would die for what she believed, along with her men. Since they would die even if she went with Johin, she chose to remain with them to the end.

"Though I walk through the valley of the shadow of death, I fear no evil for Thou art with me…" She heard Nathan recite. It was a psalm from the Holy Book. Somehow the words filled her with comfort she could hardly comprehend. He turned to her and spoke. "Ai, you must run away with the Bamish king to the borders. It is our only chance at keeping you alive." Michael said nothing but took a fighting stance.

"Stand down, you worm. What can you do for the princess in that state?" Johin said to the knight with evident irritation. "Come now, Ai, I shall protect you. I shall take you to Bamah where you will surely be safe." He urged desperately.

Ai ignored him and stared at her opponents who were now a few feet away from them. She made up her mind to willingly surrender if given the option, deciding that no more blood would be shed on her account.

The horses stopped right in front of them, and the men dismounted. Ai was gladdened that they did not pull out their swords and thought it was a sign that there was room for negotiation.

Her heart raced as one of the men approached her. There was something familiar about him that she could not pinpoint, but before she could utter a word, he went on one knee and bowed to her. The army of soldiers behind him did the same.

"Commander of the Ore army, at your service, Your Highness." A most familiar voice said, causing the princess to gasp.

"Grandfather!" She cried aloud in sheer relief. The man removed the hood of his cloak to reveal his ageing face with full grey hair and beard.

"Yes, my dearest Ai, it is I." He responded rising. Michael visibly relaxed and Nathan sighed audibly in relief.

She threw herself into the arms of the older man, and tears of joy flowed freely down her face. Her heart swelled in gratitude to the God Who had delivered her and her men. Not only did she not need to return with Johin, but she could also return safely back to Ore, under the protection of her soldiers.

Ai, Princess of Ore

Book 2

(Love's Revival)

Coming in 2025

ABOUT THE AUTHOR

Faith Oghenefejiro Adiorho is a passionate writer and storyteller who has been weaving words since childhood. With a PhD under her belt, she now dedicates her free time to blogging and crafting engaging books that reflect her soul.

Purpose and Inspiration

Faith believes writing is an integral part of her life's purpose. She sees life as a captivating narrative where every individual plays a vital role as a unique and precious main character. This philosophy fuels her creative journey.

Connection with Readers

Faith cherishes feedback from her readers and eagerly awaits their thoughts on her characters. This exchange inspires her to continue crafting stories that resonate with people.

Connect with the Faith on Instagram **@faithadiorho**

Or connect via the contact form on The Written Faith's website:
https://thewrittenfaith.com/contact/

Subscribe to **thewrittenfaith.com** to keep up to date with new publications and more from the author

Milton Keynes UK
Ingram Content Group UK Ltd.
UKHW042036031224
452078UK00001B/181